Cucklebur Stew

To Butter
Best Wishes

Lynelle Woods Graham

LYNELLE WOODS GRAHAM

outskirtspress
DENVER, COLORADO

Outskirts Press, Inc.
http://www.outskirtspress.com

ISBN: 978-1-4787-4838-0

Outskirts Press and the "OP" logo are trademarks belonging to Outskirts Press, Inc.

PRINTED IN THE UNITED STATES OF AMERICA

Based upon a true story.
Personal names of a few are unchanged.

Acknowledgements

For the apple of my eye
Carol Denise
My lovely daughter

Cucklebur Stew

Dawning chapter of the novel Cucklebur Stew is written based (by permission of the author) upon the song entitled "Crawfish Rendezvous," written by Barry Graham 2006. Graham's personal and private lyrics are greatly respected and gently dealt with hosted by my utmost admiration. Portrayal of his creativity of characters and their fascinating surroundings has truly been an extraordinary experience.

Chapter I

Simulating the wisps in a mares' tail blowing in the wind, a scarce gathering of flying cloud puffs hung high against the deep backdrop of a fabulous mackerel sky.

Lucky fellow! The song writer in pursuit of subject matter written about less than a thousand times or more could not have ordered even if he could have, a day of more perfect weather for a marvelous voyage upon the sometime violent waters of the mighty Mississippi River.

Desirous of new and unique subject matter worth singing about, the young man thought of no better hunting grounds other than would be the broad banks along the old man river and or perhaps within its impressive waters.

Having greeted the dawn of that particular September morn with quite a burst of vitality, Graham the artist songwriter, equated his spirit with that of a shovel-nosed sturgeon.

On his short jaunt to reach the vicinal harbor, he thrust out his chest, elevated a gorgeous dimpled chin and pulled in a long breath of the river's fresh water breeze.

Right away he stepped aboard his almost new, center console day cruiser, which only a few days prior he had christened "Miss Julie", then quickly checked out all safety gear on board.

Promptly he eased her out of close quarters and began a slow embarking from its berth. At once he gathered headway, then he and his beautiful Miss Julie sped out into the Yazoo River, departing from its stow in the Vicksburg Harbor. The Yazoo River immediately made its spill from the north into the muddy waters of the grand ol' Mississippi moving southward. Now while moving relatively slower, the skipper kept his small vessel to the inside bank so as to avoid any hindrance to the larger boats which solicit much more water than did he.

Destination unknown, Graham had not set in stone a specific end to the voyage. Thus destination and time were governed by the location of the worthwhile subject matter.

However, the mid-day sun warned daylight will soon be fading. Opportunity is rapidly diminishing.

All around tug boats, transport barges, and fishing boats of assorted size and colors offered a pleasant sight to see. Massive growth of an evergreen forest richly feeding upon the black fertile breast of mother Earth were themselves food for the eyes of the passing observer. And yet, none of these sparked the slightest excitement to the creativity of the professional writer.

But anyway, the handsome artist continued to search with a fine tooth comb the outlying plains in hopes of perhaps discovering something significant, maybe even a miracle.

Glimpses of fields white with cotton ready to be harvested visually flashed through thin spots of the forest trees as his journey carried him further downstream. And although the glamorously dressed cotton bowls loaned to their rich fields' ample beauty neither were they perceived as fit subjects for his hopeful palate.

Downstream immediately up ahead and fast approaching, a sudden bend to the river's pathway caused the boatman to bring himself to a direct and smart attention which was in the first place proper for a model sailor.

And, having safety first in mind he picked up speed then moved cautiously to the outer bank and into deeper water, where he continued a steadfast watch, he then brought under his control the rapidly rising wake.

Afterward, little by little the skipper eased inward more to the center of the lanky bend, keeping an eye out all the while for merging traffic.

Soon he safely rounded the river's bend then heaved a sigh of relief, "Whoa, didn't see that one coming." At that moment even though the sun was sinking low and even so the river's pathway growing dim, Vicksburg's creative songwriter had no trouble whatso-ever in drawing into view the most alluring, the most bewitching, and the crudest subject matter definitely deserving of being written about, sang about, or even shouting about for that matter. In fact, Graham quickly penned on paper the unique scene. And once he burst into a crude bar or two of the envisioned song, and then shouted good tidings to himself.

At last, after hours and hours spent in singing the blues, a most delightful song appeared. Stark naked to the eye, there it was almost the miracle he had hoped for. But of course, the man provoked milieu was no miracle, but was indeed the most incredible setting that ever he did imagine. But be that as it may, his prepared soul was eager to receive the gift so grand of the surprising extravagance. Oh Boy! He definitely could feel a song coming on. And, yes! You could say for certain that the man was indeed ready and willing to document in verse the contents of his amazing treasure.

The pleased boatman exerted as best he could a coolness to remain as focused as was possible. Gently he throttled down to reverse the propellers. Immediately he then tossed out the lead line and continued slowly his approach to the murky bayou. After having located a safe depth in which to moor his boat "Miss Julie", he dropped anchor. For a moment's pleasure, Mr. Graham simply sat still in somewhat of a calm stupor and gloated within himself over the awesome discovery.

Upon an earlier introduction to the overwhelming feast, initially it gave the skipper quite a jolt. His heart forged an unsteady rhythm as it lashed out madly against the rib cage. Pressure upon his thinking skills built big and beautiful castles in the sky. Nerve endings in his fingers dropped dead. His poor feet suffered numbness as they slept. What recourse to take, short of dying, evaded the thrill stricken man.

Right away, he gathered together thoughts of swooning, but he dared not. That particular behavior would be much too girly and girly he was not. Also there was a divine feast to collect and embosom prior to the setting of the sun. And, so it was at the expense of precious time that his incoherent drooling took precedence over the harvest of a wealth of fame. Uncertain as to whether or not he should laugh or should he cry, the two emotions merged right away and forced into play an unexpected gale of mixed passion that soon settled down to an honest heartfelt gratitude.

Out across a swampy wilderness, resting among the bayou marsh, green with a hefty cover of cord grass an abandoned old barge floated a half pint yellow school bus.

Further on down headed inland near to dry land there's a rusted Eldorado parked about half-way up a tall fossilized oak tree.

Out back of little ol' yellow, a plank board table having two inch holes cut circular, run the entire straight of the lengthy bayou barge. Underneath the round open holes, garbage cans gulp cast off parts of boiled crawfish.

During the boils busy season, a black motley dress printed in yesterday's news clung desperately against grappling fingers of the river wind and covered the crude board service counter.

Finally, skipper of the moored boat called out to the gangly young boy who lay sprawled across the pier pretending to sleep. "Hey! Five bucks for a row in." At once the leather brown pretender leaped to his feet, slid the holding line to the flat bottom skiff upward over the wharf's pile. Then in a bit of a hurry, responded to the river rats bargaining.

As the artist stepped from the flat bottom dogger and onto the wooden wharf, he thanked the boy for his kind service and tipped him the promised currency.

Then while moving in a short distance closer to the old gentleman who sat with the back of his chair leaned against the rails to the boardwalk, he spoke softly so as not to startle the napping fellow. "Good morning," he said. The weird old man turned his head from side to side, raised his facial whiskers upward and within the moment his devilish eyes were air born in search of the sky above him. Then he again turned his attention to the song writer and in doubt asked, "Is it?"

"Yes, sir," Graham replied, "I'd like to ask you some questions sir."

"Might not get an answer," snickered the elderly gent. So against the old fellows toying, Graham bravely commented, "Who are you sir? What is your name?"

"Higginbotham," He spoke in a boastful manner.

"Where were you born Mr. Higginbotham?"

"Well, now let me see."

He squinted his puffy eyes, rubbed his thin protruding chin kind of hard then replied, "Now, I believe and I think I'm correct on this one, yea, I'm sure of it! I was born crawling backward like a silly ol' crawfish somewhere down on the bottom of the Louisiana bayou." "Seems to me," said the old man, "it must have been pretty close down there to some little crawdad hole."

Quickly he scrambled to his feet and while holding fast to his chair he began to chant in a somewhat dry and offbeat rhythm.

You get a line and I'll get a pole,
Honey,
You get a line and I'll get a pole,

Babe,
You get a line and I'll get a pole,
We'll go down to the crawdad hole.
Honey, baby, mine

"That's very nice Mr. Higginbotham," Graham said. "But could you sir, tell me when you were born?"

Unfortunately for the artist, his interview of the fine gentleman had been tuned out colder than a dead man's heart beat while the strange man wiggled his skinny behind and knocked together his bony knees in some old fashioned dance he sort of recognized as the southern Charleston. At last, near to be completely exhausted, Mr. Higginbotham sat down, jumped in with both feet and began again to chant the second verse to his zany tune.

What you gonna do when the lake runs dry,
Honey?
What you gonna do when the lake runs dry,
Babe?
What you gonna do when the lake runs dry?
Set on the bank and watch the crawdad die.
Honey, baby mine.

All of a sudden, the old fellow's chin dropped to rest against his chest and his snore began to ripple the breeze that passed kindly beneath the narrow nostrils.

Anyway, Graham soon realized that he had been cleverly out-smarted by the foxy old timer. It was now quite evident that Mr. Higginbotham, at this moment, cared not to air the past with anyone, therefore, the artist simply pulled up a chair, took a seat, and waited.

Scenes round about him revealed a silent story. The small yellow bus had served Commodore Higginbotham and his wife Prudence, along with their only child, a son, whom they named Juniper, as a home for a very long time. And, peculiar as it may have seemed to some folk, the Kentucky migrates were happy with the life in close quarters.

From the exact day of their arrival to the swamp of the Louisiana bayou, native Cajuns named the three migrates "the squatting crawfish dabblers". Right away of course the fair skinned Higginbotham's were considered to be anything but Cajuns. They were, however, three Irish bred Kentuckians in search of flat lands and sea air.

But what did any of that nonsense have to do with the price of apples? Nothing else mattered; the enchanting bayou was to Commodore and Prudence Higginbotham the humble home for which they had been searching.

The adventurous couple also lucked up on a deserted school bus perched on tall stilts and was also blessed with a flat bottomed fishing boat which remained tied to a pile that assisted in the holding together of the hand rails of a narrow boardwalk that bounced softly over the bayou's crest and crept endlessly among the green cord grass.

In passing them by, commercial fisherman always enjoyed pointing out the amusing half pint school bus and its unusually pale inhabitants as being their detrimental competition.

"Look, there they are! The crawfish dabbles!" And caught by the river's wind, the hecklers tease could be heard far down stream as they raced out of sight. But who cared, the boy Juniper merrily waved them by with a pleasant chuckle of his own.

During the off season for dipping crawfish, Commodore allowed the doors to the yellow school bus to be opened in service to preacher Dumileck and his Cajun followers to use as a spiritual meeting place. Women of the bayou referred to preacher Dumileck as Brother Jack. However, since he was himself an Elvis impersonator of a sort, the young Juniper thought the name Jack struck a rather flat chord.

Daily upon first sight of incoming flat bottomed boats that were being manned by local riffraff, the boy Juniper immediately got the move on, rushed outside, flung with great strength the hand woven latter crafted of smooth cord grass over the roof top. In haste, he looped the opposite end to the wheel well and as swift as the flow of the Mississippi River, he scrambled to reach the rooftop and then dropped himself down to sit where his long legs dangled over the edge.

While his calloused toes wiggled and curled with playful joy and fragrance of the bayou flower stuffed his nose, his gripping stare sailed along the shores, gathering unto him splendid dreams of a lavish someday.

Father's unforgettable tale of a long ago mansion echoed inside his head. He scarce could place its massive size in his youthful imagination.

Sometime the dream seemed to be more of a pig in the poke than truth, but Juniper held on tight to his faith. No doubt, inheritance of the family mansion would someday surely be his ticket out of the Louisiana bayou.

Meanwhile, inside of the yellow school bus those praises which were being sung to someone that he had not yet met nor was anyway likely to. Especially down here in these parts of the forgotten world was no interest to him at all.

At the boy's present age, he was totally oblivious to any promise of heaven or hell. For the moment he'd much rather dream about things that either could actually be seen, felt, smelled. Therefore, for as far as he was concerned, the glory bound could get there all on their own, just please leave him out altogether.

Anyway, for him, he already had all that glory stuff worked out. Yeah, someday in the near future, he was going to live in a great big ol' house in the far distance up there somewhere in the mountainous state of his dream, "Kentucky". Already he could just feel it in his bones.

Much changed from his mother, Prudence, and his long suffering father, Commodore, who deeply loved the marshy beauty of the bayou and confessed that they never wanted to leave. The restless son, Juniper, received with total honesty their way of life for what it really was; drafty and wonton. Consequently, he could hardly think of anything more than that of his much anticipated escape from the bore of it all.

Why had it not have been for the grand crawfish boils which they shared annually with a collective school of the Mississippi River traffic and the wild burn on his tongue that radiated from the hot savory red peppers and Cajun spices worked up by a great chef (his father), he would have long ago grown massive fins like those of a giant fish and swam away to Spain's distant seaport Gijon.

Shortly the propped chair in which the old man was sitting suddenly slipped and the jolt bumped him back to the land of the living. Following a brief convulsive spell of laughter, Mr. Higginbotham then managed to pull himself together again and the quiz resumed.

The artist, Mr. Graham, stood up and faced his subject. "Sir, how long have you lived here in the school bus?"

"I rightly don't know," was the gentleman's frank reply.

"Do you know how old you are, sir?"

"No, I don't," he whispered.

He looked troubled. His eyes saddened.

At that pitiable moment in time, now believing that the old man could recall nothing more in any clarity, other than that he truly was born and now is; prompted the researcher's departure.

But yet, as he turned to walk away, Mr. Higginbotham called to him. "Sir, I do recollect something that's worth recollecting."

"Are you going to tell me, sir?"

"Are you going to listen," Commodore chuckled.

"I am, sir."

And so began the old man's story. I think maybe I must have

been seven or eight year's old when someone, my father I think, or it could have been my great grand dad, or perhaps my great uncle. That part's not clear, but they took me on a very long journey to visit some kin who lived far away in the hill country in the state of Kentucky.

I recollect very plain that I stayed overnight in this huge white mansion. Black folk made our breakfast. The house smelled all through it of baked apples and sweet cakes. I didn't sleep at all that night. I was too busy lookin' and sniffin' and thinkin'. That day, the story related by Commodore Higginbotham was actually the building of his young son Juniper's exasperating fantasy. Never could the magic of that exciting story be erased from his youthful memory. After having heard his father's story, he thought within himself someday that big ol' house is going to be mine and mine alone.

Now being the fast growing lad that he was, tight walls of the small half pint school bus had begun to close in on him just as the bayou sand slinks in and completely fills the crawdad hole. So did the squeeze of his half pint home feel to the grown up Juniper.

Chapter II

Over time Juniper's parents, Commodore and Prudence Higginbotham, both old and worn out from hard living, died of swamp fever.

So at the beginning of that particular time, Juniper was a very lonely and unsettled seventeen year old. He at once fell back to an earlier dream, a dream not yet forgotten over time. One that he had held on to from the first time the legendary story fired his fantasy.

Therefore, right away the lad boarded up the faded half pint school bus. He tied again the existing flat bottomed boat to the hand rail of the well-kept boardwalk then exactly as his folks had found them, he left the entire works, half pint school bus, one flat bottomed boat and a snaking board walk to others who would repeat their folly and they too would claim it for a home of their own.

Soon Juniper Higginbotham deserted the floating school bus, hailed a hitch with the captain of a shrimp boat and headed up the mighty Mississippi. At first the bayou squatter settled in Johnson county Kentucky. From Johnson County, he would begin the search for the southern mansion that had too long crimped his mind. The wait to fulfill his driving fantasy was long and toilsome to say the least. Many years passed and still all he owned of the glorious plantation was a vivid memory. Year after year he passed through many farms and cabin homes on the lonely road to claim his fame and glory.

Finally the year 1888 brought to the life of the pioneering Juniper Higginbotham who as a young man had served much in the capacity of a slave to others, great change.

Soon to rise above the wretched ordeal of his southern poverty, he at last looked with eagerness beyond those sorrowful days and into a clean face of a rising future full of gladness. No longer did he endure the need of living under a roof owned by someone else, nor would he ever again plow their fields or groom their horses simply to earn bread to eat or to earn soap for the purpose of scrubbing his body.

Not more than a week or so later, on a lovely clear day in early spring prior to Juniper's marriage to the Mrs. Higginbotham, he received in hand the legal document declaring Juniper Higginbotham to be the rightful and current owner of the post war architectural delirium.

At last at the age of twenty-eight, he found himself with a new and wonderful wife and the unfathomed task of rebirthing a doddering antebellum structure that should God give him strength, he would soon call home.

Juniper Higginbotham got busy; very busy.

But little did he concern himself because his darling wife whom he addresses always as 'Mrs. Higginbotham' was forever present at his side. She was his rock of ages and also the soft down that pillowed his head.

Juniper Higginbotham the new proprietor of Red Ridge Acres declared it to be so poor in nutritional value that it's only worth to be considered was in the small part it still played in holding the world together. Weathered remains of the rural home once bearing the sparkle of white paint now cracked and peeled to almost a non-existence sat closely edged upon an overgrown ledge sometime referred to as the red serpent, hardly earned the right to be diplomatically registered as land. But be that as it may, still its streaking acreage chased a long very narrow ridge into a pool of poke berry red clay and in its on merit, hung tight to the universe.

Extreme soil erosion devastated the lands' small bits of plains therefore offered no promise of future farming.

The once maintained road leading into the royal premises had been long ago forsaken. However, an overhang of musky dine vine and blue fox grape composed a sheltering arbor so profuse that its natural beauty formed a true diamond in the rough unlike any ever designed by a man. The magnificent utopia covered over the clay indenture the entire length of its long run of red wash. True, a great eye appeal for this extravagant green wonder beat feverously upon the covetous brow of a patient Higginbotham heir. And although he was recorded on the long end of a slow tapering line of Higginbotham heirs, eventually through the calendar count down of time and the tedious elimination by death of previous successors who for whatever reason never cared to place their claim on it, Juniper, son of Commodore Higginbotham became soul heir and he rejoiced.

Historically, the fine old building was typical of the smaller houses that were built by yeoman farmers. Architecturally, it was an actual copy of a larger mansion. For as long as he could recall, oh he would say "since I was a young boy". He had admired what remained of the historical legend.

A remembrance of true stories that were woven into history by his father Commodore and other close relatives regarding confederate soldiers taking refuge inside the southern mansion penned quite an enthusiasm to his memory. Also, other tall tales of an abundance improperly related by some were always cleaned up and quickly polished by his father; because, nothing but truth pertaining to war or family affairs was good enough for the innocent ears of his growing son. Consequently, from the very first introduction to the fine old remains, Juniper had admired its endless wonder.

At the present time, here in the midst of Juniper's good fortune, a sudden notion invaded his joy. A longing for the nearness of his mother and father caused him sadness. And the realization of having no siblings, no not one, lay heavy on his mind. He experienced the marvelous blessing of having his dearest wife, the Mrs., to share in his pleasures but he now misses the family whom he once desired to separate himself from. Oh, the foolishness of youth! Anyway, life goes on. And, with each passing year he envisioned himself as a fine southern gentleman living within its walls, as the wealthy overseer of a bustling house filled with lavishly dressed off-springs, as well as himself and enjoying a splendid life of ease tended by lots of pampering slaves.

Often the vexing dream emerged from his imaginary mind so clearly that his faded casuals appeared to him as white linen trousers. His straw hat frayed and dirty became pure white and banded like a gentleman's formal straw. The work gloves worn on his rough and untidy hand transformed themselves to pure white silk which dressed not rough and calloused hands but fine delicate ones.

But right away within that same moment, the dreamer's bubble burst and he awakened to the realities of a real world. Then at once he openly declared to himself, "Oh, woe is me, old man. Don't bog yourself down with silly notions!"

Juniper's awareness of the fact that such an enormous task of restoring the run down mansion would no doubt require the expertise of knowledgeable professionals, forestalled the determined gentleman not at all.

On his side, faith replaced financial funds and brawn tripping on the heels of brain, ran a very close race.

Guts and strong will gave no slack to the chase. And there was love.

Over time, together the two newlyweds removed most all noisy squeaks from pine board floors and interior walls. Replaced window panes, hung hand crafted shutters, and scotched the slight tip of the mountain stone chimney.

Once on one blessed occasion, and most fortunate for the Higginbotham's, out of the past came a few friends who had in deep earnest searched high and low among hindering thorns and thistles to find them both still in one piece. That wonderful day the expansive gable roof received new shingles.

Following an over night's rest for their guest, the new day rolled in on a low drift of milky fog. Rising up from the valley, a dense fog seeped silently through tree tops in whirls of angry billows. Mountain tops sank from sight in humble surrender to its fascinating hunger. Millions, it seemed, of black mosquitoes danced huddled together in giant wads in likeness of a kitten's hair ball. Dampness brought in by thick fog tended to chill the bone even in the warm month of June. Working conditions were threatened. However, the clever man of the house balled up and burned old rags outside then rolling clouds of smoke chased away the vicious insects. All the while, Mrs. Higginbotham kept the black coffee brewing.

Cup after cup mixed with cream and a spoon full of sugar or once in a while either cream or perhaps only sugar, continually passed the sipping lips of those who toiled. Then occasionally someone of them called for simply a mug of the hot strong black undiluted pure stuff; an eye opener indeed.

Next day, the work crew, who from experience of their own chose the cool of the early June morning to shell out their all in the correcting of the aged antebellum's second story hanging balcony. Somewhere along times' pathway the hanging gables veered a bit too far to the left. Consequently in order to properly bring it back in line to the massive entryway, new rods made of hard steel were in demand. So, thanks be to Juniper the chief blacksmith himself and the fine crew of volunteers, the back breaking mission soon was accomplished. So having squared away their intended task, old friends who once were Cucklebur citizens folded their tents and returned to a less hostile environment, leaving the proprietor and his misses all to themselves to complete the ongoing endeavor.

One day at a time, the eager couple labored almost nonstop, working their fingers to the bone and enjoyed every moment of it. But even so the once elegant structure somehow lost its original design to the ever swinging pendulum of time and failed miserably to recover much of its maiden glory.

By and by in her appearance, near the finish line, she sort of took on a mimicking look of her inherited inhabitants. Rather poor but sturdy.

Rejuvenating columns replacing the elaborate ones were not ornate or gilded to depict their majestic era, but were instead cuts of fallen chestnut trees.

The huge round trunks were fallen in March, the season which rendered easy stripping. During this time of changing seasons, bark readily released from the mother trunk. Afterwards, they were cured by the summer sun, and then painted buttermilk white.

Juniper himself hand crafted strong exterior doors, but creating stained glass in a blacksmith shop proved totally impossible. Hence the clever hang of the plain and simple architectural barricade transposed rural harmony.

Inside the house, walls also were totally innocent of the elegantly embossed finery. Once again in lieu of superior vintage wall coverings, wide boards cut from very large cedar trees gathered from Red Ridge itself sealed them.

And so upon ones entering the parlor, a vicious fragrance almost shocking immediately greeted the open nostrils and provoked an instant inward outcry from the visitor. Cedar!

No matter, due to many obstacles, such as distant hazardous travel and unpredictable elements, few guest seldom entered through the Higginbotham's broad and gay threshold.

Still other deviations from the original décor took place. Electric lighting generated by a large quantity of a solid compound of an element, usually a metal with carbon called carbide, stored in a very big brass vat and buried in the ground somewhere outside the enclosed structure, took the place of oil burning lamps.

Light fixtures themselves gave way to their surrogate of abandoned wagon wheels, and wooden yokes that were once worn by domestic oxen. Thus because of an abundance of them, those sorts of fixtures easily replaced the elaborate ones which were stolen long ago by heartless vandals.

Juniper's handy motto of 'there is more ways than one to skin a cat', always quickly spoken, seemed to Mrs. Higginbotham to be just about as heartless as the thieves who stole.

"My goodness," she exclaimed also posthaste. "Who in his right mind would want to skin a poor cat?" Nearly always Mr. Higginbotham avenged her heckling repartee with a flirtatious hug for his impish misses.

Finally after months and months had gone by, at last renovation of the inherited delirium now called home, had been completed. And so, like a giddy child, Mrs. Higginbotham turned the silver key to unlock the front door. The glorious occasion arrived gracefully on a cool September evening.

All around, colors as soft and enchanting as those observed in the surprise of a rainbow were closing in on summers green world. Bitterness of summer times angry soring temperatures had begun to mellow. Over worked and in like figure, so were the muscle bound Higginbothams.

Anyway, little did it matter because the husband and wife had both reached the end of their lengthy and difficult task. Therefore, Juniper's long coveted harvest was now in the bag.

While the happy couple was being led hand in hand by the argent foxfire of a big round moon which hung like a gilded Zion above them, he and she together proudly stepped a few paces back, front and center, to the lovely sparkle of white buttermilk paint then at once prepared to pay a proper and worthy homage to their long difficult labors. Although, the once upon a time grand and noble fantasia was far removed from the renowned southern home it once acclaimed. Still, to the fine couple Mr. and Mrs. Higginbotham, it measured up quite well to their expectations. After all, family warmth and comfort came first on the new owner's agenda. And warmth and comfort no one could deny.

Henceforth, Juniper promptly recalled the old adage of 'a man's home is his castle', and then he reared himself straight back, way back, thrusting his round melon-like belly forward and with both giant hands began to drum out a hollow sounding ditty to accompany the thunderous chuckles that followed.

"Mrs. Higginbotham," he bellowed. "My dear, standing there right in front of you is our castle; yep, yours and mine."

But suddenly the boastful laughter sobered. He then quietly tucked her small worn hand gently inside his own hand and with a most honest and open feeling, pressed it to his warm thirsty lips. Right away, by the passionate display of his desires and the unmistakable heat pouring from his longing, loving eyes, his misses could not have misread the cue had the card hung upside down. Again, remarkably soon, Juniper Higginbotham got busy; very busy indeed. Within the first fifteen years of the couple's marital bliss, their revamped antebellum home exploded with an honorable count of twelve fine southern born offspring. Of course, Mrs. Higginbotham also had a pretty steady hand dabbling in that specific affair.

However, Junipers' previous dreams of having silk and satin to clothe his children was just that – dreams. Nor were their pampering slaves to nurse and tend their every need. Those days of what the old folk referred to as the days of wine and roses had long since gone by. Juniper was a considerably poor blacksmith and he had learned a very long time ago that dreams do not in no way pay the piper.

Somewhere along their prestigious pathway, the Higginbotham wealth had fallen through the political cracks.

Notwithstanding, he a pleasant man of honor had been innocently entangled in the web of monetary poverty alone. In the character building attributes that really count, love, respect and honor, his pockets jingled. Also, and in spite of his past afflictions, he had come to think of himself as the man whom he had once envisioned himself to be; a wealthy southern gentleman. But, although his stalwart appearance, oft times denied that vision, still he insisted upon holding firm his vain imagery.

Even so, he was known to rule well his very large household of six sons who had a sister each his own. Peace and harmony almost always reigned supreme in the Higginbotham home. And of course, the apple of his eye was none other than his adoring wife, his misses.

Many years long before Juniper Higginbotham inherited the narrow ridge farm and had come to live there, the land had already been brutally ravaged of all its fertile top soil by years of wicked erosion. Burdensome efforts to replenish the devastated farm land hardly seemed worth all the back breaking efforts required. Hence, during planting and harvest seasons, because of the want for workable land for themselves, Juniper's children, boys and girls alike, excluding their youngest sibling "Brother", all found work as hired field hands working in the neighboring fields down in the low lying valleys.

Since Brother was last to be born into the Higginbotham bunch, and was also considered least for the most part in all family attributes, it seemed most reasonable that he needed no formal name for identity purposes. Brother adhered to him at birth just as firm as the southern weed beggar's lice sticks to cotton.

Accordingly, fat chance the poor guy had of ever outgrowing that pretention. No matter, Brother rather enjoyed the great height of his honorary pedestal. Furthermore, perhaps just maybe, the wee baby was never meant to be tagged by a given name such as Bill, Jim, or Joe. From the very beginning the sweet name could have simply been providential. But, only the hearts of each sibling could understand. Actually it was neither here nor there what the lad should be called. The need to call him at all seldom ever arose. Always he seemed present and accounted for. From birth forward he never strayed far from his mother's site. Anyway, each of the boys had a sister of his very own, which brought the grand toll of Higginbotham children to an even dozen. But neither one of the remaining eleven was as overly protected and regaled by the entire Higginbotham brood as was little Brother, which ultimately tied him for the most part of his life to his mother's apron string. Rare moments when his mother found spare time to sit for a pleasurable moment, Brother was forever pressing her comfort while childishly wallowing his blond head on her shoulder.

If and when mother stood at the sink to wash dirty dishes, Brother invariably held tight to her dress tail and trampled on her already aching feet. Sometimes on rare occasions, when she lay down in hopes of enjoying a short nap in the afternoon, Brother lay snuggled close beside her and twisted her hair.

And so it was, although Mrs. Higginbotham's love for her baby boy ran deep and undying, oft times she felt as though perhaps instead of a precious son, she had mistakenly born a blood thirsty leach.

Many times her constant fears ran rampant among dreadful worries that maybe this painful worm had claimed a permanent position buried deep within the confines of her flesh. And then Mrs. Higginbotham chuckled within herself at such weird nonsense.

Year by year while the youngster stretched his luck in growing toward adulthood, his overblown ears which somehow so well simulated the wings of a butterfly at rest, got thumped way too often by his older siblings, especially those of the annoying male gender. Even worse, the little guy's roman shaped nose received a playful twist many times a day. Further still, the poor kid's skinny rump was either back-handed or squeezed which ever seemed appropriate at the time to whomever the transient culprit might be – much too much. Likewise entirely too many crushing hugs, all freely given in the name of love, pretty near stunted the boy's growth and encouraged an even closer knit than before to his enduring mother.

Nonetheless, it was but the passing of only a very short time it seemed, then Brother too, very much like the older brothers had grown up and he himself followed in their footsteps and also became a notable equestrian. A profession he acquired out of necessity and not exactly for the love of the sport or past-time.

Forever, down through time, the young horseman had longed to mix it up with the rough and tough brothers before they outgrew him altogether. Even so, bearing that dream in mind, Brother watchful still kept his riding range close to home and close enough to keep an eye out for his mother. Nevertheless, consideration of the lot of burning trails and growing pains, Brother agreed with himself that it made no difference to him how many or how few scrapes and bruises he might or might not collect, or even how many tears he just might need to wipe from his eyes, the climb to the top would be worth it all.

Eventually, the painful climb uphill all the way did by some miraculous way, pay off. Little Brother now at the age of sixteen is at last acknowledged by his teasing peers as a courageous fellow, 'a real man'.

"What a price to pay," exclaimed his mother. One day midst a very warm dry July evening, sheltered by a dreamy cloudless sky, the Higginbotham boys were all harvesting field peas for a gentleman farmer called Jason Ironwood. Mrs. Ironwood employed their sisters up at the big house.

Anyway, Juniper, his Mrs. and Brother were at home keeping watch over vital necessities there in the hill country; near the hour to expect the working children to come home, oh, usually around four or four thirty - seldom ever later than five o'clock. Most times it would be right on the wings of the busy fireflies that were out to light up the night.

Brother and his father Juniper hustled off toward the blacksmith shop where they would build a fire in the forging pot.

On their return home from the fields, the young sons would need plenty of hot embers burning so they would waste no time in forging out new shoes for the hoofs of the horse. The tired men would also be eager to call it a day.

Chapter III

U pon a sudden moment's surprise, a most unusual noise came to Mrs. Higginbotham from outside the front door. It was not a simple knock. Nor was it the sound of a bang or shallow scrap to Mrs. Higginbotham the stridor was sort of baffling.

At once she dropped the knitting needle into the basket, folded the incomplete sweater across the arm of her chair and turned a more intent ear toward the front part of the house. She strained her ear to listen but not another sound arose from that specific direction. "Am I simply hearing things," she asked herself. Curious, the lady of the house moved forward and with some caution approached the huge barrier.

Slowly she released the forged iron latch and eased the door opened to a mere crack. There through the small opening, Mrs. Higginbotham saw lying on the door steps, sprawled upward from the bottom step to the top step, face down, quite a poor excuse for a man.

At the tips of his long lean fingers, lay loosely a lengthy knotty pine bough that had some time ago fallen from an evergreen tree. It was on that sturdy branch that the strange looking man had dragged his wounded body for a great distance. The crude walking support also served him as his means to gain the attention of Mrs. Higginbotham. Prior to loss of consciousness, time allowed the poor fellow only one opportunity to make his presence known.

And so accordingly, the one erratic thud produced by the butt of the crude cane, supplied for the fallen stranger, the needful alert.

Shocked by what she observed, right away the lady of the house called out as loud as breath would allow, the name of her husband, "Jun-i-per!" Fortunately for the frightened lady – help was already on the way. The Higginbotham daughters had already left behind themselves the home of their employer and headed home when the cry of their mother rang out. As quick as a flash, all six girls bypassed their father's blacksmith shop, took the trail running down the lovely shady lane and then sped like race horses through the open gate of the long fence row – then home.

Brother's great stride placed him close behind. The young adults found their mother busy patiently bathing the lips of a wounded stranger.

"Come!"

"Don't be afraid," she coaxed. "He needs food and drink."

When brother observed the lifeless skeleton of a man, his eyes came to a sudden rest upon bushy eyebrows dark and streaked with gray, dramatically arched above deep set eyes. The wayward man's small and beady pupils glared blindly through drooping eyelids. His dirty hair shown as black as crows matted feathers, receded and tumbled thick across an unusually narrow crown. A straggled beard, black and heavy masked an out thrust chin. His flesh although sun exposed appeared waxen and dowdy. Full lips dried and cracked by over exposure to harsh elements, enveloped teeth worn thin and uneven.

Furthermore as Brother continued the vigilant inquest into the unclean transient's crane like, uncontrolled neck and long lanky legs, he burst into a belligerent chuckle and declared, "Well, my Lord, Ma! If I didn't know any better I would surely think this poor old soul was old Abe Lincoln himself. He's the spitten' image of the old departed President." Perhaps we now have royalty on our hands.

Remarks of foolishness were always expected of Brother. Foolishness made up his flamboyant character. His mother smiled a reluctant smile. His sisters laughed out loud.

"Shush", Mother instructed, "the gentleman is injured, not deaf. He will hear your snide remarks and be insulted. Now, make yourself useful and get him inside."

Furthering the compassionate part of her character, Mrs. Higginbotham advances with instructions regarding goodwill to her children. "Spread a quilt on the parlor floor." The lesioned torso was much to fowl with odor to lay him on the family's bedding. "At once fetch a pillow from the blanket chest", Ma continued.

Just then father Juniper stepped inside the humming parlor. Soon after receiving a complete explanation regarding the stranger's presence and the full account of how he frightened Ma. And all about how Brother mistook the tall lanky specimen to be Abe Lincoln, Juniper cleared the room of all females then he and Brother went straight to work. The two acting Samaritans cleaned the gentleman's wounds and freed his soiled body of a full crop of summer's caked crud. Following all the tossing and tumbling done to his fragile body during the course of his purging, at last old Abe, as Brother dubbed him, slowly came around.

Although the weary travelers festering wounds appeared to the eye to be only scrapes and bruises, one could very well tell the gentleman was in great pain.

"Who are you," host of the house implored.

The visitor gasped out two words, "Ho Bo".

"Where do you hurt," Juniper again asked. Following a rather long pause, finally the weakened man exercised every ounce of energy that he could possible manage, then inch by inch moved his boney fingers to fall across his swollen ribcage.

"Good Lord, broken ribs", grimaced Mr. Higginbotham. A cumbersome wool jacket frayed and dirty covered the man Ho Bo's miserable torso, therefore, Juniper was unable to actually investigate for himself and so he ask, "How many?" Ho Bo replied with a painful strain, "Five of them as best I can tell."

At once by Juniper's demand, the suffering Ho Bo was moved to a bedroom next door to the kitchen and made as comfortable as was at all possible. Straightway he was administered nourishment of food and drink that was prepared by the hands of the young ladies residing in the refurbished mansion. Hot chicken soup soothed the belly's cavity. And a sip of Brother's elderberry wine warmed the blood. And father Juniper said, "Pay proper attention to him, my daughters." Perhaps later on if it should seem necessary, we shall locate the good doctor and invite him to come to our aid. "I'm quite certain," said father, "we will find him somewhere in the close proximity of our sister town, Paintsville."

Following Juniper's proposal, Ho Bo moved his head side to side in protest of Juniper's suggestion.

"Doctor, no! No," he groaned.

But the lady's father paid little attention to the stranger's objection and continued on. "My daughter, make sure he is kept warm and clean. See to it that he is well nourished. His recovery now rest within our hands. We must go now," said Father, "and leave him to his rest."

The door to the hobo's bedroom was pulled almost shut but not quite, so the Higginbotham family cleared the room leaving him with his deserved privacy.

Thereafter the mysterious stranger, except for food and drink, refused all offers of anyone's favor in preference of caring privately for himself. Although healing time became rather lengthy, the need to summon the doctor did not arise.

So as was Brother's custom, he kept always in the background, not too close neither was he far away. Father thanked his family for their cooperation and said. "He will be residing here with us for quite a spell." The daughters all received their father's instructions with grace and it was so.

The very thought of leaving the house entirely to the Ho Bo's discretion burned at the very core of Brother's soul, and so he the suspicious one kept a tight rein on the comings and goings of the visiting stranger. Strange thing about that endeavor though, was that poor Ho Bo never even made a single attempt to leave his room.

But anyway, still each time the door to Ol' Abe's room stood the least bit ajar, Brother somehow found it necessary to often pass it by in hopes of catching Ho Bo in some devious deed. But as always, the convalescing fellow remained quite as a house mouse.

Nevertheless, unknowingly to Brother, Ho Bo built himself a strong fort of awareness against the wilds of his young self-appointed guardian's careful wonder. Therefore in like manner, his sportive eye trailed every move of the Higginbotham spy with much amusement.

Brother kept very close to his mother at all times. Even after all these years, he had not yet cut the apron strings. But, not to matter, Mother was of the utmost importance to her baby son. He held her in his highest esteem and it was no secret as to who the kind soul was who, buttered his bread and fluffed his pillow where he laid his head. Had it not been for Ma, he never would have made it to be full grown.

Between the twisting of his rather peculiar nose, the spatting of his bottom side and the unbearable squeezes given him in the name of love and for all the scrapes and bruises he received from learning to ride a merciless horse, it's a thousand wonders that even his mother could have saved him.

But, Ma was always there to supply plenty of healing kisses. Now it's his turn to roll out the red carpet in honor of his sweet and trusting mother. It made no difference to the young man called, Brother, that he had been tagged "momma's boy". He wore the petty name with pride for the sake of his mother.

Always and until his dying day he would be willing to endure trials and tribulations coming from any source in order to protect the one he loved. And in no way, shape, or form did he ever consider himself above prodding, poking, or even dying so as to keep the old mansion a safe place for Ma. And in reality, Brother was secretly admired by the entire household for his true gallantry.

Father Juniper especially placed his son very high up on his list of honorable children in spite of his occasional uprising frustrations. Mrs. Higginbotham understood the well-meaning characteristics of her twelfth born and truly adored him for who he was.

A great deal of time passed. The rise and fall of many suns and moons became to the wondering Ho Bo only a memory. Days, weeks, and even months bloomed and flourished.

Then just as beautiful as were their flowers, so was the withering and dying away. All the while the wounded swagman, familiar to the Higginbotham family only by the name of Ho Bo had occupied a place in her home almost mute, deafening quite. He spoke when spoken to, not one word more.

"Good morning Sir", said Brother.

"Morning," his guest replied, neither suggesting the morning to be either good or bad.

"It's a fine spring day today, don't you think?"

"Fine," was his single remark.

"Are you feeling better today?"

"Some."

"Good grief," snorted Brother to his Mother, he's awfully complex, almost barbarous. Presently realizing how thin Brother's patience had worn with their guest, Mrs. Higginbotham shushed him outside.

"Now, now, son. Please take the broom and sweep off the back porch." But even then, a curious strain of the ear to what might be going on inside annoyed him to no end. Uncouth as the weird guest may have been, the man himself simply rubbed his nerves the wrong way.

Nonetheless, a little further on into time when he at last did speak each and every resident of the Higginbotham household stood up, took notice and held on tight to each and every word. Cogent or meaningless its worth counted not at all. They were all especially eager to remove the dark mask that he had insisted upon wearing for so long.

Over time by gathering to mind a few words here and a few more there and aided by the gentleman's few one liners, Juniper soon summed it all up in a nut shell.

Like a pieced coat of many colors, he, a very clever man pieced together the untold story that had daily been sung by his long time house guest. It seems as if the unnamed hobo had been chasing behind a fast moving engine of a freight train for far more years and more miles than he really cared to count.

And it seemed also that it had been his lot in life to claim a moving boxcar as home. Quiet evident, dust and grime from the steel tracks had faithfully provided sweets for his sweet tooth which revealed untidy teeth. Garbage dumps and dirty trash cans placed along life's byway had generously fed him. Far too frequent hard liquor had been his drink.

It happened while on his last binge that he had fallen from the open box car onto a graveled bed lying aligned to the hard steel rails. And while under the impairing influence of strong drink he mistakenly believed that the train had braked to a stop.

As he leaped from the moving car, the tattered sleeve to his woolen coat caught and held firm to a projecting iron peg. The poor hobo was then dragged a long distance down track before freedom eventually came to him. Unconsciousness blinded him to the exact location of the painful deposit.

So, as best as his memory served him, he thought perhaps it was possibly somewhere outside the small town of Cucklebur. However, he somehow recalled to memory of having viewed an abandoned coal yard along the way which would have placed the incident to have occurred further south of the town of Cucklebur.

Juniper himself believed the stranger had made his way from somewhere along the eastern part of the Appalachian Plateau. That being true, the laborious journey could not have been all that far from the Higginbotham plantation. After all, first off, the location from whence he came did not make much difference to the lame hobo. Nor did it matter in the least as to where he would be going. These subjects of interest, springing up inside the mind of Juniper, seemed off limits and intolerant to the house guest; therefore, the discussion of the matter closed pronto. "Weren't going anywhere anyhow," snorted Juniper to himself. Juniper's final assumption of the man's poor attitude toward life brought him no joy. He was a man of indifference. He simply gloated on the idea of being here one day and somewhere else tomorrow. However, at this point, his journey had not been so swift. Hard luck had thrown a whirling rod into life's speeding wheel and brought the foot loose and fancy free hobo's travel to a squeaking halt.

At last upon the end of the twelfth month period of his stay, a new day dawned for both the Higginbotham family and also for their injured patient. That lovely day appeared as a gorgeous spring flower bursting into bloom. The soft sunlight filtered deep down into the morning's dew and gently dried it all up. Encouraged by the warm gay light, Mrs. Higginbotham passed through the broad expanse of the antiquated dining room and headed upstairs as was always her customary practice. Once inside the girl's sleeping chambers, mother's melodious yet sharp hail awakened the slumbering six.

"Good morning my herd of angels, rise and shine!" But today the customary decorum differed. Immediately her attention fell upon the stately carriage of their house guest seated in a chair that he had taken liberty to pull away from the long trestled harvest table.

At once her rushing feet felt to her as though they glued themselves to the floor. The halt came so sudden that she almost toppled forward. On purpose, he faced the east wall of the sunlit room. Narrow cresting shoulders and a very straight razorback spine held the lady's stare. Turning neither left nor right he ignored her presence and kept right on with his concentrated gaze as though she were not there.

His outstretched fingers still showing strong bones appeared to be caressing some light weight tool. They moved in sporadic motions not clear to just what might be their intentions.

Also an occasional straight forward lean followed by a taught fling of the right arm forced Mrs. Higginbotham to judge the man to be somewhat mentally unbalanced.

"Good morning," said she very gently. Again, Ho Bo ignored the missus and so momentarily she herself felt as though she was the stranger in the house and began again to walk toward the stairway.

"Wait," he shouted.

"This wall," said he, "refuses to speak to me!" Certainly those irrational words no longer left any doubt in her mind as to the state of the poor fellow's mentality. He indeed is daft.

Forthwith she became fearful of him. "Must I call for help," she asked herself. "Or would merely a soft word turn his wrath?" However, a quick turn of her head toward the room's exit and she spotted her son Brother casually leaned against the doorway's facing.

Yet unaware of the lady's fear, Ho Bo inquired, "It's rather bare, don't you think?" Right away as she is too confused to speak, Mrs. Higginbotham finds herself to be the mute one. Now although she had heretofore regarded herself to be a woman of perfection, those evil assumptions regarding a stranger brought her shame.

Once more and this time, quiet deliberate, the recuperated hobo stood up then turned to face his friends. My realization is that your humanitarian benevolence has far exceeded my imagination. Consequently my greatest wish is to repay you with a pleasurable and lasting token of my most sincere gratitude. At that moment, Brother hurried to release his shoulder from a lean against the door facing then proceeded to make known to all concerned, the burr under his saddle, he took a firm flat foot stance.

"Well," he loudly exclaimed. "The dead man has risen and spouting highbrowed words that no unlearned man could speak. It would be pretty interesting to know, simply for the sake of knowing; just what sort of box car school did you attend? And another thing of interest to me is have you a degree?"

"Who are you?"

But the gladdened hobo ignored his rude attacker's challenge and continued on with his proposal to the lady of the house. "I wish to leave you dear lady with a living wall that will speak to you. Now that I have recovered from my wounds and will soon be parting your company, I wish to get on with my labors right away."

Brother's roar once again leaped from wall to wall. "And just how exactly do you purpose to bring this miracle about?" The two immediately moved closer together. Their eyes met and locked in a competitive gaze. Yet, Ho Bo's mellow voice remained calm and controlled as he began his reply.

"By creating an eloquent mural that will fill even your soul with a sweet narrative more beautiful than any tongue can tell. One generously engrained in brilliance of color and light yearning always to tell the love story conceived deep inside my heart.

"But you old man have no paints, no brush and not even a landing to stand on", cried Brother.

"So that, my dear boy, is where you come in." At once the hobo settled himself again in to the chair to face the room's east wall. "If you agree dear lady, I shall need to cover the entire cedar board wall with canvas.'

"Canvas, canvas," snorted the faithless Brother to himself, "and I suppose out here in the forest he thinks canvas grows on trees!"

Going on, Ho Bo drew their attention to himself by a brief thrust of his chest and a somewhat unsavory stretch of torso skyward. A squelched groan followed. "As you can see, I am very tall; all of six and one-half foot. Nevertheless, I am quiet shy of the twelve foot height that is needed. Therefore I shall be required to build a sturdy scaffold." The artist then turned silent and looked to Brother for an affirmative reply. "Will you please assist me in that matter? But, my dear boy, as to where I shall obtain proper supplies of paint and brush, you need not concern yourself. I shall myself pay special attention to those particulars."

Evening of that most unusual day, all too soon wrapped its uniqueness inside blue blazes of sunset then rest it's weariness upon red clouds going down. An ongoing mystery residing inside the Higginbotham household had resolved, sort of, in part. The day's end returned Juniper once again to his home. His labors at the shop were laid to rest so that he could do the same for himself. Upon receiving remarkable accounts of a most impressive day, he quickly approached his mysterious house guest and said to him, "My good man, you have made my misses a mighty happy lady. And when the missus is happy, so is the Mr."

A little belt of humor was meant to liven things up a bit. But to poor Juniper's dismay, his humor was met only by gloom. So he hastened on in search of an excuse for living. "Such things, fussy things, such as art and music have forever met my women's fancy. But, due to constant consideration of her children's needs during hard times, opportunity to enjoy those things did not knock."

"Alright then," exclaimed Ho Bo, "as both you and Mrs. Higginbotham are in agreement, I presume I am free to begin sometime on the morrow. But first I have an impertinent request."

"Yeah, here it comes" Brother remarked silently. "I knew there was bound to be a fly in the ointment somewhere."

"If you please sir, will you honor my need with the loan of your son in constructing the necessary scaffold?" Brother's resentment came down so powerful on his own tongue that his teeth drew blood. "Also and again, I shall need to borrow a horse and buggy for a swift trip into town."

The hobo's reasonable request met with Juniper's trusting approval. Brother, however, was neither trusting nor approving. Instead, he himself felt more or less betrayed by the father in whom he did trust.

"Only," began Juniper, "I do suggest you should take Maggie, the brown spotted mare. Maggie is much more docile than any of the other horses and she works very well on distant trots.

That special night, the whole world lit up like day. Overhead, stars subdued by the brightness of the moon stole a peak here and there through the parting of an evergreen canopy. And so it was, by the silvery glow of a harvest moon that Ho Bo rode off alone dressed proper in loose fitting clothing once worn by the considerate man of the house.

Although the two gentlemen differed quite a lot in body weight, their loftiness varied little. Consequently for Ho Bo his luck ran smooth. All the while as the man Ho Bo rode away clippity-clop, feeling the freedom that he had almost forgotten, he marveled at all of nature's glory.

A brief thought of the boy, Brother, he left behind gave to the night's ambience an easy chuckle and puckered his thin lips to whistle. On through the lovely night, Maggie the mare carried him riding smooth like warm butter while pressing against the cool breeze that lapped playfully at his borrowed finery. "Oh what a night," he whispered in pleasure.

Brother's suspicious gaze followed Ho Bo all the way down the long strait, where skies, although moonlit, darkened beneath Mother Nature's massive green arbor and quickly shut out his sour vigil. Even though Brother's lack of faith in the stranger's return drew a blank, fear of his father's wrath gave him a reason to pretend.

Very soon it was Friday. Gone already a night and day and to this point in time Ho Bo remained sight unseen. And so was Brother's favorite horse and buggy. Bitter visions of the hobo's disappearance and thought of his taking with him his prized possession ulcerated inside Brother's churning brain. Needless to say, Brother's temperature was sure to be on the rise. But father Juniper's faith in his fellow man withstood the odds.

On the late eve of that next day, as a reward for his patience, Brother's father was glad to welcome back to the mansion the lumbering bones of the tall, thin stranger and all his necessary cargo. A quick eyes inventory revealed two large rolls of plain white canvas. Stacked to one side of the buggy were two-gallon cans of oil base paint to be used for the killing of the background. Also, there were small boxes filled with tubes of a large array of colored oils. More boxes contained paint brushes of almost every size and shape that could be manufactured.

Brother's favorite buggy over ran with a heavy load of every needful thing that the slated project could possibly require exclusive of a wooden scaffold and that of course Ho Bo himself was compelled to build.

So, since the hobo did indeed return fulfilling his promise, Brother the doubting Thomas was forced to re-pocket his laid up, well versed, "I told you so".

Meantime, Ho Bo exclaimed, "Oils on this side of the Mason Dixon line are difficult to trace. Likewise or even more so is superior canvas." Amused, Juniper chuckled to himself. Conscious of the territorial town's brand of entertainment, he understood very well where a big part of Ho Bo's time was spent. Nevertheless, the old fox enjoyed as much as any other old fox, tall tales.

Anyway, Ho Bo's return was just as promised. On the morrow, he however did not specify exactly which morrow. But, all is well that ends well. Excitement beamed brightly from the deep set eyes of the artist. He immediately went straight to work. His assistant tried to hide but failed and so he too went to work also.

In no time at all, the indoor scaffold grew to a perfect climb. And having supporting aid of an able bodied young man, pushed the project forward rather rapidly. Brother detested every moment and cringed at the very presence of the mystery man.

Ho Bo's fingers itched at the thought of once again stroking with oil a virgin canvas. It would be within his painting that he would live again.

Therefore, presently introduced as an artist, he climbed steady upward toward the towering ceiling of the southern mansions east wall, a familiar and welcome emotion ascended upon him. A long longed for return to his world, made for him a very happy day.

By his hand a pale gray paint killed the enormous back ground in its entirety. Drying time of the cover then allowed a short rest for the artist. That night while the entire house slept, the hobo seized the moment and made himself busy by very lightly drawing in the planned subject. The following day he slept.

At this time, the subject of the painting remained a secret to all residents of the Higginbotham household. Meantime, among the entire family there was a whole lot of guessing going on. Juniper's daughters unanimously predicted in all confidence that it would be a field of lovely flowers. Juniper himself believed that it would surely be a stunning portrait of Anna, his fair lady. Anna, his missus, re-garded herself too proud to make an assumption of any sort, simply placed it all in the creative hands of her friend Ho Bo and prayed. All but one of the six brothers hoped upon hope that the stretched out canvas might literally spit out girls, girls, and more girls.

Of course Brother's only desire was to have no part in the stranger's uproar. So because of his bottled up resentment toward the artist, he simply begged the pardon of all concerned parties.

So pleased to have been given the opportunity to now at last prove to those skeptics who looked after his needs thus far, that even a hobo can sometimes be useful, day by day he exercised with pleasure his remarkable talent. Again and again, over and over his fingers long and bony like those belonging to a skeleton encircled sometime the small, sometime the plump handle of the well-turned brush and made it to dance over the huge canvas as graceful as a magical swan wherever the wings of his creative spirit found it needful to fly.

Oft times whenever Ho Bo lost himself amid the rise and fall of shaded shadows and then suddenly found himself again entangled among the grainy pigment of color, he sometimes appeared to those looking on as a total mad man.

Momentarily while soaring heavenward when caught up in such fiery fury, the artist becomes oblivious to his present surroundings, to thunder, to lightening, and even to the beauty of a falling star.

"Insanity," declared the voice of the Higginbotham watch dog. Who, I implore, in his rightful mind could display his emotions in such a pitiful fashion? Often when the artist retreated to bed, Mrs. Higginbotham stole a quick peep whenever she happened to stroll through the parlor foyer.

The young ladies of the house were very much impressed and excited by the creative manifestation of their extended visitors love. But, each of them took great care not to disturb the creator.

Time moved on. Dramatic change came daily. Suddenly, or so it seemed, from the east wall of the Higginbotham dining room, once cold and silent, a majestic sunrise reached out with its brilliant lights, red and promising a fair day. However, the day with all its thrills far surpassed its promise.

Actually, a fair day turned golden. A bored wall once plain and naked at last wore the diamond studded crown she well deserved. She now speaks through lavish strokes of multifold colors and high-brow words in example of those often spoken by the artist to all those who dwell in the house overseen by his friend Juniper.

Finally, work of the unknown artist ceased. Right away he took leave from the work place and immediately placed himself directly beneath the lofty archway and turned to face the master piece. Once more driven by force of habit he held in hand the point of his heavy bearded chin and while feeling no reservation whatsoever, approved the stronghold of his sweet alms for a sweet lady. Instantly a pleasant and easy nod accentuated the positive.

During the present hour all the house pealed peace and quiet; other than a ticking clock in every room.

A windy night had cleared rain clouds and brought down a peaceful purple sky. Daybreak hung close around the corner. Hence, Ho Bo harbored no qualms in awakening the lot of them. "People, come quickly," he shouted in loud demand. So startled by the early hail, each Higginbotham young and old alike, hit the floor running. Four young ladies clad in sleep ware rumbled down the somewhat shaky stairs creating the sound of a herd of cattle. The two older girls were no longer living in the Higginbotham mansion. All four ladies stood with their hands sucked up inside the long sleeves of their night gowns and their arms folded snug across their chest. Each of them rolled their sleepy heads pressed against the parlor wall and waited to hear the punch line.

Only half of the six Higginbotham boys remained under the roof of their father Juniper. The other half had already shuffled off to Buffalo. The three who stayed behind in residence, bumped shoulders playfully, pushed and shoved at one another as they fought for personal space in the crowded hallway.

Never before had they heard the quiet voice of their guest so firmly pronounced. "Is it fire? Is he dying," they all wondered. Urgent, it was indeed urgent, but neither fire nor death did reign.

Upon the family's prompt arrival, Ho Bo coaxed them each one to gather around him. "Come near, this is a celebration." Presently stilled and slow to awaken, they each one observed the slow easy movements of the now proven artist while he signed in dark umber his name, "Fullerton".

"Fullerton," Juniper read to himself.

Then again, "Fullerton." He loudly exclaimed.

Everyone's lips came unglued and every chin dropped in awe.

Fullerton, Fullerton, Fullerton! Somehow Ho Bo's revealed name, his given name, Fullerton, the real name became as much a celebration as did the signing of his magnificent painting. That is, Brother being the exception stepped up forward from his favorite leaning post against the back door facing shouting insults that curled the shoe clad toes belonging to his father.

"Fullerton! Van Gogh! Mosses, or Christ! Dress him up in any name you please and he will still be nothing but a mooching hobo."

Brother had there-to-fore very well hidden all his ill will toward Ho Bo from his father until now. His mother, as mothers do, felt the annoying misgivings eating at her resentful son, but only in part. She thought they were only growing pains and had no clue as to its depth. The whole of the Higginbotham clan near fainted from shame.

As much as he was adored by each of them, at that moment none could bare to look him in the eye. Brother, on a moment's whim had scattered to the four winds their family tradition of kindness, honor, and just plain ol' respect to others, especially to visitors in their home. Brother trembled at the unpleasant scene. All around the lovely dining room grew as quiet as the fall of a snow flake and just as cold, even though spring beat upon the door. Still holding on to a bit of a smile that previous joys regarding his gift of love had induced, Mr. Fullerton seemed to receive the outburst to be no more than a common occurrence. Soon he turned to address the lady of the house. "If you please dear lady, I would like to exchange for the attire I wear, to those of my own. I trust you did keep them in reserve?"

"I didn't burn them if that is what you mean," the lady smiled and Ho Bo rolled his eyes. At once, the missus scurried from the dining room and across the parlor hall and then into the bedroom of her own. A rosewood blanket chest, an antique inherited from her maternal grandmother, placed at the foot of her bed held the clothing Ho Bo had worn upon his arrival. The artist frowned upon the neatness of them.

A thorough wash and pot boiling made a very dramatic change. They were clean. Still, he in an appropriate silence took the shirt, the trousers, and the long woolen coat from her hands, taking care not to allow his glance to meet her lovely smile.

In something of a nervous rush, the hobo then entered the room adjoining the kitchen that he had for many months reckoned to be his and at once changed from Juniper's fine clothing into his rags not so fine.

On the nightstand that he had pulled together side by side to serve as a much needed desk, he laid down the small paint brush he had used in signing his masterpiece, still clutched in his hand. Soon after all the others had cleared the dining room save Mr. and Mrs. Higginbotham and their intolerable son, Mrs. Higginbotham soothed the overwhelmed nerves of her much perplexed husband merely by touching his hand. Immediately Juniper followed the lead of his missus and softly spoke to his son and said, "Son, you have my permission to leave the room if you so desire." Brother accepted his father's sufferance with gladness and did so but not without first leaving his calling card of stubborn arrogance. "Well," he mumbled under breath, "a man's gotta do what a man's gotta do."

Prior to rejoining his host Mr. and Mrs. Higginbotham, Ho Bo the artist stripped the linen first from the feather pillow and then the bed. He then stuffed the soiled clothing and linen into the pillow case. "I must leave the room tidy," he whispered to himself. An afterthought then moved the stray paint brush from the desk and into the cardboard box placed beneath the bedroom's only window.

The large box stored unused supplies left over from the dining room project.

Right away, Ho Bo's departure began. He picked up the bag stuffed with laundry and placed it near the doorway. He then immediately rejoined his angels of mercy in the foyer.

Strange thing, no expression of a fond farewell in any form occurred between them. No hand reached out to grasp another. No head gave a single nod in sad adieu. Not a smile or a tear drop to tempt the other.

The quite vagabond simply walked through the open doorway and closed the heavy barrier behind him. While standing motionless on the top door step, in silence he surveyed his amazing surroundings. The changing season set a miraculous table in color and in style. Autumn had begun to sweep away all traces of summer and its musical notes. Songs of the green katydid and of the brown cricket are rapidly winding down. The reveling grasshopper now has danced his final performance. But, leaves of red and green are yet to recite their poetic prose and soften the season's transpose. The splendid moment's pause in time recalled for Ho Bo his dramatic arrival to a perfect heaven and he smiled to himself a comforting smile.

And at that moment's reflection the nomadic loner was persuaded to pinch himself so as to confirm that actually the bones contained in the package of rags could be those of his own.

Suddenly, he leaned himself steadfast upon the crude cane that brought him to the Higginbotham revamped mansion and once again dressed in the same tattered rags he wore when he arrived. Ho Bo the artist commences the sore and tiresome journey back into the common life realized only by the homeless.

Slowly one foot is placed in front of the other. On and on each foot replaces the one before him. Inch by inch the toilsome tract is eaten alive by its persistent chaser.

Off to the east, a red blaze from the rising sun calls out the name that is real to him, Ho Bo. And he replied, "Here I am. Don't fret yourself Mr. Sun. I'm back on track. I'll be there soon."

Back on the other side of the closed door, Mrs. Higginbotham marched straight down the hallway and immediately entered through the open doorway into the recently vacated room which once housed a very mysterious man. Anxious to amend the bedroom's content, the lady could not believe her eyes. They were seeing a very tidy nook. Mr. Fullerton had restored a lost faith in the human race. Right away she approached the bedside table which Ho Bo himself had neatly put back in place. On the table lay a gorgeous railroad pocket watch. A gold chain coiled in neat circles around the gold open-faced time piece.

Fearful that the hobo had left it there by mistake, the missus carefully picked it up and rushed down the hallway, across the parlor, and quickly out the door in an attempt to overtake her house guest. However, the limited speed that old age afforded simply cut the time short. She called out very strongly but her guest had already slipped away. Juniper came almost in a run from the back porch to the front porch to examine the ruckus. "I fear", said she in a shortness of breath, "Mr. Fullerton has by accident left his time piece." She then passed the fine pocket watch from her hand to Juniper's hand. Juniper gazed with much perplexity upon the exquisite gold watch.

"Yes, Mrs. Higginbotham, this is a very rare Bunn and Bunn Special," his remark seemed curious. Mrs. Higginbotham seemed even more curious. "You see my dear! These aren't purchased by just any ordinary gentleman; they are made by special order especially for railroad engineers." Going on, Juniper said, "A Bunn and Bunn time piece is the longest ticking watch without needing to be wound daily that exists today. Don't need to wind it but every two and a half days. All others need a daily wind."

"My goodness my dear," Mrs. Higginbotham exclaimed. "How

do you know so much about a time piece when you don't have one of your own?"

"I saw one once, just like this particular one. It was among the treasures of my great grandpa's possessions years and years ago."

The old couple marveled at such a great wonder and together pondered the soundness of Mr. Fullerton's ownership of the valuable treasure. Finally Juniper whispered, "My dear, I am of the strong persuasion that it was no accident that our friend Ho Bo left us this valuable time piece."

Afterwards, the old man kissed the cheek of his sweet missus and then with great care considering its value returned the hobo's fine gift to her gentle hands. "It's just another gift of love," she softly whispered. Soon afterwards, she pressed the ticking time piece to her ear and then to the ear of her husband and remarked, "It's ticking sounds like the beating of a heart."

Yes, Ho Bo's heart", Juniper said while wearing an easy smile.

Straightway, Mrs. Higginbotham's small but spirited feet moved the grateful lady across the hallway, and the parlor, then directly into the spacious dining room.

Just as Ho Bo promised, from the east wall a brilliant light glowed, warming her soft face and spoke to her. "Come in fair lady and share with me, this pleasant day." At once she moved to the east end of the harvest table near to the magnificent oil painting. Void of any doubt regarding the stranger's worthiness, his grateful hostess then laid the gold railroad Bunns and Bunns Special in the center of the hand quilted placemat and said, "This is the place that he himself refused to claim, but henceforth, here at our table is where our hearts shall beat together, Ho Bo's, Juniper's, and mine."

Speaking in a soft whisper, Mrs. Higginbotham said "no doubt we shall miss our dear friend, but I am certain that someday, somewhere, somehow, life will be good to him. Juniper echoed the sentiments of his missus, but couldn't help but remind her, "Dear, no man is an island, we aren't meant to live alone, therefore, if Mr. Fullerton is searching for a lasting happiness, he must seek out a wife, settle down and shave off that confounded beard!"

Mrs. Higginbotham chuckled, "Juniper Higginbotham! You do brighten my day!" Right away as means of warding off the unpleasantness of her good friend's departure, Mrs. Higginbotham rushed out to the compacted clothes press which stood at the end of the kitchen's hallway and began to sort through old linens in search of those fit for making of a lovely quilt. Juniper slowly and quietly drifted off to the blacksmith shop where he just might do a bit of cleaning. Do note, however, that no firm promise of cleaning was made and of course you do realize that mites grow under a chicken's wing.

Chapter IV

(Ten Years Later)

Over time the cold winds of constant change swept through the happy corridors of the age old southern home. All at once it seemed, Juniper's children were all grown up and in want for offspring of their own. And so as nature required of them, each went their own separate ways into the outside world; one daughter, one son, two daughters, two sons. One after the other until all but one of the twelve had parted ways. The five sons immigrated north in search of better education. Of course, someday, beautiful wives would also fit into their plans. Also a small selected serving of a controlled adventure was certain to find its way to each of their plates prior to his settling down.

However, daughters of Juniper and his missus each chose either north, south, east, or west. Their choosing depended upon the moments dream. Most were drawn more to the idea of meeting a wealthy husband than that of furthering an education. Thus sisters of the six young men's route of departure flowed more to the west. Gold miners, ranchers, or mercantile proprietors could by all means appease the thirst of a girl longing for wealth.

Each young lady did indeed share their father's dream to own mansions, slaves, and fine dress. Accordingly, to the dismay of father and mother, their daughters traveled over land and sea to faraway places. Some had strange sounding names. Others were plain and simple like Maine. Poor Juniper wept.

It appeared to matter none to anyone that Brother too was full grown and also in want of a wife and children! Differing none, it remained quite obvious among his siblings that it would still be Ma's apron strings that would hold him fast.

Much too soon, both Juniper and his lovely missus had been overtaken by fleeting time. They now were old. Light in their eyes had dimmed to near going out. Brittle bones were of great concern and pain. Vital strength for both was almost spent. Neither Ma nor Pa could any longer care for the other. So Brother determined the urgent duty to be his and his alone. And, perhaps since his decision met no opposition what so ever from his careless siblings, he at once realized that it was he whom they endorsed all along. Be that as it may, Brother counted it a privilege and not a chore.

Shortly thereafter, Juniper died. Four short weeks later, his missus sank deep into a grief like quick sand, and then died. Brother's labor of love ended far too soon. He himself now bears a consuming grief. The mansion he once adored now is bombastic and shudders underfoot. The evergreen forest surrounding his home closed in and its natural beauty appeared to be nothing more than a very dark insult.

Ho Bo's magnificent sun rise refused to give off his brilliant light to anyone. The east wall to Ma's happy dining room again slept in the darkness. Ho Bo's masterpiece no longer spoke to him. His whole world fell mute about him. Despair knocked at the lonely man's door. Yet, he like the Bible character "the prodigal son" came to himself.

Hence in due time following the long endurance of a morbid winter of freezing ice and snow that was driven by a mourner's song of howling winds, Brother made himself a promise. I will arise and again walk with earthly pleasures. I shall leave this my father's house and build a cabin of my own. Then I shall marry myself a loving wife. A fine women like my mother, patient and understanding. And he said, "It will be to this woman that I shall with great delight surrender all. Henceforth in my cabin home she shall be the eastern wall that speaks, and to me she will forever be the rising sun." Soon afterward, many children will be the dance to my woebegone feet. And I shall be to my children a happy father.

He went directly to work on previous plans to build for himself the promised dwelling, much smaller than his father's house, yet spacious enough, where he in the likeness of his father Juniper would marry a wife and fill it up to the brim with many offspring.

Immediately, but with a reasonable measure of patience, he walked over the entire considered plot of land in search of the perfect sight on which to place the cabin. In doing so, Brother carefully considered first of all the northern wind's steady current. Should the cabins door face north as to take advantage of the winds cooling current in the summer time or should it face south where it could absorb every ounce of warmth from the southern sun during the bite of winter; an important factor to be considered indeed.

Brother's long lean portion of property came to a very abrupt finish on the north end by a broad flat front which ascended mighty steeply. Rough and frank in manner, yet enormously beautiful in structure, it measured in depth two hundred feet or there about. A huge outcrop of blue mountain stone naturally stacked over on top of the other offered a dazzling overlook to an enchanting valley down below.

During the search, Brother's cautious footsteps placed him near the bluffs drop. He looked down. His inquisitive eyes instantly fell upon a gorgeous sea of golden grain swaying unfettered in the wind. Further on, leaving the glory of the valley, deep dark shadows draped themselves like soft down blankets over mountains dressed in evergreen trees. Their rippled contours simulated peaceful rivers of easy flowing waters.

Kentucky's wild deer stole away from the thick of brush, embarked unafraid upon the open valley and helped themselves to eat of the farmers golden oats.

This was not Brother's first visit to the great bluff, no, not at all. Many times prior to that moment he had observed the sublime view but never before with a true feeling regarding natures beautiful gift.

That day his heart opened wide to the thought within himself and he said, "Often I've wondered where God built the Garden of Eden?" Afterwards he felt certain of the answer. Immediately, Brother concluded, the cabins front door will swing outward toward Eden. And so after having squared away the precise location to build up on, Brother Higginbotham clear cut the chosen spot then journeyed back to the old southern mansion to await the coming spring. In other words, he specifically waited for the coming month of March and Mother Nature's rising sap. Taught by his father Juniper all the specifics regarding the nature of trees, Brother understood rather well that the chore of debarking trees came much easier following the sap permeation.

Down through time, among the Higginbotham clan, the Farmer's Almanac counted for a very dependable weather prediction. Thus for the upcoming month of March a poetic recording of "in like a lamb out like a lion" caused no concern for worrying on Brother's behalf. He simply waited.

And during the long waiting period housed inside the old home place, Brother passed off the cold winter days by packing dishes, iron pots and pans, bed linens and box after box of flower seed. Seed saved over time by his mother, perhaps too old to germinate would be to some folk worthless, but to him they represented his mother's hands. Anyway, the anxious bachelor put to good use every valuable moment. He longed to make simple the forthcoming transition.

By and by when at last spring did come, she arrived with a smile on her face and bringing with her all of her glorious fullness. And in language of a gung-ho seaman, earth bound Brother hit the deck a running. He peeled from his back a heavy bundle of winter apparel, gathered together all the necessary tools that were needed to raise a log cabin, one bow saw, one broad axe, one muscle driven auger, plenty of wooden pegs, and an abundance of pure manly grit.

At once while sporting a new and adventurous spirit, he headed north directly to the far end of his inherited ridge. Entertainment along the long journey provided by the natural pulse of nature stormed the door to his heart and advanced to his lips a sensational pucker which produces a pretty rabid whistle. Following after him would surely be his good fortune; a fortune that soon would surely renovate his driving notability.

And so it would be there on the peaceful soil of his red ridge mountain, enclosed by the symphonic composition of a far distant waterfall and blessed by a golden sun by day and the silver of the moon and stars by night, he a mere pilgrim of time would live, love and be happy forevermore.

Juniper Higginbotham, III filled most of the present day with the falling of sugar pine trees, but the debarking of them rounded out the remaining hours of the very busy day. Poor Brother's back ached, his hands wore huge clear blisters inflicted by their exposure to fresh pine rosin which continuously oozed from the fallen trees. His feet were swollen and his head began to throb. All of these manifestations of age caused him to stop and consider how time does fly. Meantime, while in deep thought regarding life's calamities, Juniper never let go of his dreams. He did however reconsider the counting of chickens before they hatched. That special spring and summer came then disappeared much too quickly. Much too many unfinished chores hung in the balance for another year. All the same, early fall returned Brother once again to winter at the old home place on red ridge. Upon his arrival, Brother was slow and cautious to enter the old antebellum. It's taxing door, weighty with dampened moss squeaked like the door to a haunted house. Breath of the lonely mansion smelled of spoiled milk. Its hasty touch to his face, cold and brazen, forced the wail of icy tears to fill his sad eyes. At once he observed the silent stillness to the long ago voice of Ho Bo's master-piece. The emotive brilliance of its once florid reflection today sinks out of one's sight and hides behind utter ruin. Mud dauber wasp and their flawless organ pipe habitants are cemented communal style all across the painted canvas in its entirety. The nesting insects' showy gold mines, even though they themselves are a genuine work of art, deprive the masterful painting of its earthly value and rob it of its divine glory. Also spiders in their silky flair draped fine webs for themselves, corner to corner, top to bottom, while constructing their fatal cities

What's more the love fed sun will rise no more with a mischievous twinkle in his eye, nor will the east wall of Ma Higginbotham dining room ever again speak to anyone. Although Brother Higginbotham diligently searched out even the lowest corners of his heart for the smallest grain of respect for the mystery man, artist, hobo, who knows, still somewhere down deep lurking in the cleavage of his soul, he felt a vast loss regarding a strange man's brilliant creativity.

But more than this, Brother clearly recalled the daft occasion on which Ho Bo presented his proposal of the gift of life to the east wall of the dining room. And, he recalled very vividly with a bit of resentment the unforgettable glow it brought to the sweet face of his dear mother.

"This wall refuses to speak to me," resounded the recalled voice of the hobo. "It's rather bare, don't you think?" Brother also recalls Ho Bo's going on and on about his wish to repay the family for all their good deeds done toward him, and all about his own strong resentments and suspicions regarding strangers.

Anyway, poor Brother cleaned as best he could space enough to meet his needs during the wait for the coming spring.

Toward the end of this another winter season, he had begun to take on an unwanted feeling of a hermit, a pathetic loner, a loose recluse. In spite of all the busy notions floating around inside his head, the quite loneliness somehow snuck in. Brother Higginbotham marveled each passing day at the enormous labor that his ear was compelled or driven by simple hope of collaring one single unit of sound, the sound of life – a life of any sort. It could be that of only a chirping cricket or a croaking frog. The screech of an owl would be most melodious to the ear. And, oh yes! Even a scurrying field mouse or two would be a joyful noise.

Day after day, the restless recluse engaged a slow but steady hand in the task of crossing off in black ink the days which numbered the winter season on his well-worn calendar. Three long months were recorded, December through February. Oh, yea. A truly rhetorical log of time did in fact abound and suffered very little kindness to its harboring captive.

Brother counted every tick of Ho Bo's railroad watch. But its steady ticking seemed worthless. Crucial days dragged on. Finally and at last, by the hair of his chinny chin chin the month of March huffed and he puffed until he blew – oh no! Hold your horses. It happened quite the contrary. On that terrific day there appeared no huffing or puffing of the wind, no howling in the clouds and not one house dismantled. Those made of straw, sticks, or brick or any other kind did not fall down.

Rather and instead, that precise month of March breezed in exactly as a lamb. Cool, calm, and collected, just as the reliable old farmer's almanac predicted. "In like a lamb". Of course, it's going out, yet undone, could certainly be debatable. Like a lion? Or, like a lamb?

Very early the next morning, Brother Higginbotham began the

lonely exchange with a bundle of nerves and a heap of mixed emotions. Today's transition from mansion to log cabin would be final. His mind was made up. There would be no turning back.

At once he began the force of strong will by grasping in hand his mother's apron which hung from the back of a kitchen chair and with much tenderness of heart, he hung it back on the wooden peg on the kitchen wall where she herself had placed it. Now and again Brother had worn the apron himself while kneading yeast bread. Already, days ago, he had boarded up the windows. And so quickly he bolted shut the massive door, then hitched Maggie, his favorite mare to the buggy which once in error he thought Ho Bo had made off with, then with grief moistened eyes, Brother rode on toward a more conceptual world. And for a sure means of wiping aforehand guilt from the slate and to also drown his many sorrows, the pathetic man broke into a most heretical yowl. Even Maggie the mare flinched, as though her flesh had met with some bludgeoning blow. But her smooth trot remained tactful.

Far down the long narrow wooded ridge, a fair good ways view, Brother observed humbly his new home swallowed up by the fall season's ripened sage brush. The silver sage glowed beautifully in the early morning's light. One would actually suspect that diamonds had gone awry and came to rest upon the field. But their striking beauty found no u se to the new proprietor. The sage brush had to go.

There was work to do and plenty of it. No time to waste on trivial pleasures such as silver sage, diamonds, or day dreams.

Other than sage brush needing to be moved, there was a great need to rock wall the fresh water spring. A barn to shelter his beloved Maggie was impending and most urgent, the building of a chimney to the cabins' structure prior to the fall of winter. Also, fresh food must fill the root cellar.

But not to fret, he, driven by great intention, a willing mind, and the day's present needs, blazed the trail. That day while wrapped in the comforting arms of a sky far more blue than is the ocean, a renewed spirit revised a sad heart. The evening's arrival to his new home made Brother glad.

Therefore, to the long ago hobo; he lifted high his cup of cheer. "Here's to you old' man where ever you are! May the mischievous colors from your paint brush and the ravenous light from your sunrise ever flood your soul."

Chapter V

(Fall 1928)

Thus one event paramount in nature, took place during Brother's most impertinent time of establishing his own turf. He had barely noticed the sprouting up of a new town not more than ten miles away. The sudden town "Cucklebur" acquired its name and very fittingly from surrounding fields of corn which lay practically all together overgrown by the southern weed Cucklebur.

Soon, talk of rail traffic on the rise spurred a small swarm of establishments to gather together in and around the rumored location. In a very short time thereafter, the lively town Cucklebur came into full bloom. And with its beautiful blooms came also greed. Among the commercial community every merchant small and great hungered for rumored coal fields possibly as near as their nearest neighbor Paintsville located in Johnson County.

Straight away, gullible merchants established trade centers and mercantiles on only a floating pretense. But Brother Higginbotham did not join them. He refused to wear loose feathers in his hat. He, a very wise man, knew that with the first jolly poof of wind, his hat would surely be featherless. Furthermore, he did not relish the destructive gorge of the gorgeous landscape. So, as he thought on these things, in the presence of a collective silence, he declared out loud, "I am happy with who I am and I'm content to wear the honorable title of blacksmith" He said progress is good, but a happy heart is better. Hence, let come and go what may, I shall stand on my own two feet.

But the very next moment, the boastful echo of his own cry came back to haunt him. He heard the whisper of a little voice inside, "Marry a wife, father children. Marry a wife, father children." A taunting promise once made in all honesty, to himself, again resurfaced.

Very quickly it seemed and autumn faded in the distance of time. Shortly thereafter the fast approach of winter rallied Brother's fear of yet another lonely and chilly season. But lucky for him what to do swiftly foreshadowed winter's fury. "It was soul searching time! Strip down naked! Bare yourself for an honest stock."

Need for a kindly woman, still there. Want for offspring, holding fast. A heart ready for love, quiet intent. Dreams worth the chase, genuine. A willing mind, unbridled. Now, my man, what say ye? Let's clean up this mess and get on with it!

In light of the soul's shakedown, Brother soon realized his wants appear to be holding the upper hand. The lovely idea of a soft warm female body lying asleep in bed next to him seemed mighty rewarding. Immediately following that beautiful vision, Brother closed his smiling eyes and shut tight his ears in a playful pretense of shutting out the sound of a whole house filled with running children. Ah, what a dream. "Please! Give me more." The next morning, feeling cheerful and eager to give his romantic wings a try, the dream driven mountain man prepared himself for the upcoming scenario.

So as the means to deliver this soap scrubbed handsome dude into the waiting arms of the luckiest girl in the town of Cucklebur, he chose his father's frisky horse rather than Maggie the faltering mare. In age sweet Maggie had grown a little beyond the capabilities of performing a task as important as this one.

Rocky, a more dependable and stylish horse would assist in promoting his fantasy much more to his liking than would his Maggie. However, regardless of age and faltering feet, sweet Maggie would forever remain Brother's favorite. Just the moment Brother commenced his mount to the back of Rocky the horse, a curious thought burrowed his mind. "Brother," he exclaimed. Then again, "Brother, how on earth can I ever introduce myself to a fine young lady as Brother?"

Never before in his memory had he considered the chummy tag of "Brother" to be any kind of a bother to him at all. Not until now and now is the time he regards as crucial. Repeatedly he grunted an inward disgust at the juvenile nickname. And yet, by the same token, he cried out in praise to its bonding power within his family unit.

Given a moment to think through the dilemma, Brother recalled a time long ago when he was but a boy. His mother had explained to him the legal and rightful name his father had given him. "Son", she began, "You will always be known as Brother to your father and me and to your siblings. None other than Brother would be fitting. It makes no difference, documented in the legal system you will be addressed as Juniper Higginbotham, III. "Heavens!" he bellowed, "That's worse than 'Brother'. Juniper is just fine, but hanging on the III! Forget it! My Lord Ma! I'm the son of an Irish immigrant, a descendant of a Kentucky farmer gone Louisiana bayou crawfish dabbler. Yeah, those creepy crawling things called crawfish was main course for those swamp folk. Me and Juniper Higginbotham, III? Oh, no, please deliver me from the sissy sound of some uppity squire.

Anyway, as it seemed to be fair and proper in solving the problem he inwardly agreed with himself to take on the unworthy name of Juniper but to never breathe to anyone the daunting III. Presently pleased with the decision he had settled upon, Juniper handled alright his valuable time and quickly mounted the restless horse then rode off down the red ridge headed toward the town Cucklebur.

This visit to town would not be his first. A few times prior to this he and Maggie had sojourned on less important occasions. While galloping along the scenic way and feeling somewhat like a wolf on the prowl, Juniper began an oral rehearsal of his self-introduction.

"How do you do, I'm Juniper Higginbotham!" All for the sake of planting the rightful name "Juniper" instead of the name "Brother" on his tongue. There could be no mistake, and so over and over repeated he, the name charade. So loud and forceful was his drill that from far across the deep cut valley to the north, the magnificent tree, bearing mountains joined in his pretentious folly and returned again and again to the sender, his own dialogue unbroken.

"How'd ya do? I'm Juniper Higginbotham!" But as he had planned, he took great care to tuck fast the chiding III under his tongue. Underneath the swift feet of Rocky the power horse ten mile of red clay turned and clipped off in twenty minutes flat. He and his rider stared straight down Cucklebur main street long before they had expected to.

The strange feeling of seeing but not believing, which was nothing new to him, surfaced once again. How can it be, he quizzed, that I now live so near a town?

So near in fact that a walk in would not be out of the question.

While he pondered these strange things, an early morning breeze, a bit frisky but gentle, swept down Main Street and skipped across his square cut face then on to playfully rearrange the perfect part in his once blonde hair, now changed to a black that is darker than the feathers of a crow.

Moving on, Rocky pranced in delight from his thoughts of being a shimmering display, and on the town's main scene no less! Juniper's head turned from side to side. First left then right while his hopeful eyes discreetly searched out every probable post where some fine lady might rest. But to his dismay, none, not even one female came to his sight. Right away the reigns he held in his hand tightened then he and his horse made a quick trot in and out of the Cucklebur's short streets. Next Rocky and horseman moseyed on down Cotton Street past the cotton gin and then made a final trot to the town's square where stood the water fountain. There a brief pause allowed Rocky to drink a few swigs of cool water from the watering trough, which in Juniper's crafty estimation appeared to be the work of a crude craftsman.

Regardless, it served very well the thirst of visiting animals. All the while Rocky drank; Juniper continued the scan of his surroundings but to no avail. At last and speaking to himself, he said, "Cucklebur's population evidently consists only of old men, middle aged gentlemen and lots and lots of Kentucky peon. Now and then there were older women glued to their gentleman's side masking the earthen town's boardwalk. The many milling about peons marred the beauty of its streets. Disappointment saddened Juniper's tawny face. Time seemed wasted. Bad timing, too anxious, evenings are most likely times to view fine ladies. He whined to himself, "So, where to now?" "Home," he replied to the quiz. "I've got work waiting, but I shall return tomorrow in the afternoon."

Over the hill southward near the small town's edge, just when Rocky's wholehearted pace headed them directly out of what Juniper thought would be his promise land, he hears someone call out his name.

"Higginbotham!"

Juniper immediately pulled tight Rocky's bridle and soon slowed his gallop to a trot. Afterwards the trot mellowed to a full halt, but Rocky's frustration kept his big black hoofs prancing around in full circles.

"Over here!" The unfamiliar voice again called. Some rugged looking fellow and a pair of young ladies bunched together in front of the post office porch.

"Calling me?" Juniper asked?

"Do you see anybody elsewhere?" snapped the authoritative smart aleck. In a flash, Juniper remembered himself as being kind of short fused. Hence, a stern reprimand could easily avoid a bloody nose.

"Ok my good buddy, now calm down or you're likely to blow your stack!" And heeding his own reprimand, Juniper held onto a rallied coolness, slid off the brilliant coat of his horse Rocky, then tied him to a convenient hitching post. By and by while enduring a direct deposit of sunshine in his eyes, he endeavored an attempt to access the matter.

While lingering briefly in thought, he hooked both thumbs into the corner seams of his trousers' front pockets, leaving hands to dangle. He lowered his hatless head. Set the eyes in a sullen stare and then in a rather halting manner, kind of swaggered across the earthen street toward the threesome.

It was the almighty scalawag, Duncy Poe, a field hand of Jason Ironwood. He and Juniper had met as the two of them pulled corn for the Ironwoods a couple of summer's ago.

"Come on! Over here." Duncy pleaded. "I have some girls I want you to meet."

At once a frigid shyness cooled down what he thought to be the perfect swagger. Immediately Juniper Higginbotham dropped the performing pretense by first allowing his thumbs and pockets to go their separate ways. The bent and bowed sacroiliac returned to home base following the rebirth of a handsome face which topped out the man he should have been all along.

Juniper's re-born countenance flamed red, his heart raced ninety miles to nothing and sweat drenched the palms of his hands. Anyway, Juniper begged the Lord's mercy as he shyly continued to step across the narrow street that soon placed him face to face with the smiling party.

Duncy began to speak, "Ladies, meet my old buddy." Quickly, Brother's rude interruption served to tie up loose ends of the intro.

"How'd ya do, I'm Juniper Higginbotham!"

"But, but," Duncy bellowed, "

"No buts Duncy," Brother snorted.

"I'm Juniper Higginbotham!" Duncy didn't quite understand Juniper's change in names but he did however catch the drift. But, regarding the "old buddy" part, Juniper's brain broke into an insane dance around the charge of "Old Buddy".

He whispered, distant acquaintance is much closer to the truth. So what, Duncy had girls and girls was his main objective. "If I may," Duncy begged to continue. "This is Nancy Roe. And, this here is Hattie Clemens."

Juniper made no mistake in recognizing Duncy's attraction to Nancy Roe rather than Hattie Clemens simply by the quick way he passed over the introduction of Nancy and by the rude way he deliberately pushed Hattie in his direction.

Both young ladies were pretty enough, friendly enough, and oh so cheerful. In fact, regarding Juniper's assumption of the ladies re-spect is implored. Nancy seemed a smidge too friendly by the way she bounced around too close to the scalawag Duncy Poe. She was in no form or fashion palatable to the good taste of Juniper Higginbotham, III. The girl appeared to be as dunce as poor Duncy himself. On the other hand, Hattie, the taller of the two girls, emerged much more civil than did her friend Nancy, however, femininity failed to be a virtue that crowded her style. But anyway, at that moment, Juniper was about to make a complete fool of himself with the tomboyish Hattie, when suddenly, wham! His guardian angel came swooping in so close to him that her wing caught the roman nose of the fool-ish earthling whom she guarded and at once turned his attention in another direction.

At that very moment an angel pure and genuine appeared in the doorway of the post office. Poor Juniper's first glance crumbled him like a soda cracker. He wished to inquire of the Lord, is she really real? Might she fly away? But the gape of his trembling lips forbade the attempt. Suddenly and without any regrets, Hattie became a thing of the past. The lovely vision now present in his view made the helpless fellow stand up straight, smooth down his hair just right and wish to the Lord of mercy that he had put a decent shine on his shoes.

Now having been bitten by the love bug, previous desires to play the part of a fool vanished. At once that sobering moment turned passionate. Brother very much liked what he saw. The fine pink of this girl's cherry cheeks embellished the soft gleam of her light brown hair, cut short and brushed upward high over sudden cheek bones foreclosed on noble feelings. Juniper Higginbotham instantly fell head over heels in love. This pretty lady, no doubt about it, was the women who would in the future fill all the needs of his heart.

She is round and soft and plump like his Ma. There is a sweetness about her which rivaled the sweetness of even Ma. All these beautiful virtues, powder puff cheeks, plump soft body, and kind cheerful eyes came nicely together and wrote for Juniper a tender love song.

Right away Duncy Poe picked up the explosive attraction between the two and called to Anna. "Come on out here Anna and meet my old Buddy!"

"Oh my, there he goes again with the old buddy thing," said Juniper. But this time the insult softened somewhat while his thoughts clung solidly to those of Anna.

Chapter VI

Anna's nearness planted inside him the good seed of hope that he had at last found home. A steady courtship between the two young lovers out lived the month of January but February's frigid weather brought on a torrid marriage. Their simple exchange of vows was made on the second day of the month, while the two of them stood holding hands out in the middle of a beautiful winter field. A vast crop of purple grass enhanced the entire meadow, dressing up the private occasion in magnificent style.

Already a man of twenty-eight years old himself and Anna pushing twenty-five, Brother was completely convinced that for their cause, time was of an essence. Neither of them was getting any younger. Too much time had been spent alone. Juniper, III, was anxious, perhaps too much so to enjoy the overflow of his cabin home. On this valid point there never occurred not so much as even a hint of rebuttal. However, the over worked argument came from only one side.... his. Brother, quiet conveniently pleased himself well by a ready recall of his Father's constant quote. "You must make hay while the sun shines." Well, the sun was indeed shinning and that happy fellow could wait not another day to begin his long overdue heyday.

Within the moment, the new husband's thrilling dream pictured a baby cradle. And yet upon the mention of the subject of babies,

Anna opposed the proposal fiercely. She cried, "Already I've raised a family. Please, no more!"

During that hour of such alarming revelation, Brother could have sworn to hearing his own heart break. A more depressive spill he could not have imagined. "How could this be?" He inwardly groaned. Anna proceeded to explain. In tears, she began her sad story. Through no fault of her own, my dearest mother fell desperately ill from a chronic depression following the difficult birth of twin boys. From their birth forward into adolescence, the grave responsibilities of their upbringing fell on my inadequate shoulders. Therefore down through time the joyful experiences of simply being a little girl were for me unknown. Opportunities to play with friends my age were almost obsolete. As time moved on the dream of being wild and free ate away my youth. Even though I adored the twins and felt special to be their sister, I consider myself miserably imposed upon. Most all my days and nights were lonely even in a crowded room. I often cried when no one was looking. "No dear," Anna wagged her head in renouncement and continued on, "I must be truthful. I'm sad to say, but there is no room in my heart for any more children including those of my own."

"But, but, Anna; I'll work my fingers to the bones," pleaded Brother. "I'll leave my bed at night in heed to their cries. I promise to make light your work load. Only, please Anna, make room in your heart for only but one." Still the love of his life turned to his humble plea a deaf ear.

Anna's cold indifference regarding his appeal would now be forever a thorn in his flesh. No matter, he could never consider living one moment apart from his dearest Anna. Love will find a way. In faith he consoled himself. Perhaps someday she will come to understand.

Time rolled on.

Soon good times of bountiful living faded from the couples little cabin home. Now, not only did Brother bare the pain of Anna's rejection of having children, a serious depression seared the south-land's riches and plunged hardworking families into poverty. Food became difficult to obtain and hold on to. Food staples such as sugar, flour, and coffee were tolled out to families in rationed quantities.

Homegrown corn ground by local mills furnished bread for their daily intake. Biscuits or yeast bread they considered to be a luxury. Out of fear, neighbors were sometimes forced to bar their doors shut against each other. Legend denotes that on occasion, down south in deep rural areas, neighbors were actually sited visiting with each other while standing on opposite sides of closed doors. Also, during the historical depression of the thirties, because of the lack of proper clothing to shield them against a bitter winter, some folk suffered frostbite to their hand and feet further complicating matters already in the dire straight. In other words, the old south had again fallen not to war, but to famine.

"Hoover's Day" it was labeled. And "Hoover's Day" it will for-ever be remembered as long as the world shall stand. Eventually, because Brother and Anna owned a home of their own and most of their kinsmen were renters, they were compelled to accommodate from two to three or sometimes more drifting visitors who lingered endlessly or so it seemed to Anna, simply to be fed. The couple's crowded space soon over ran. Anna became overworked and lonely. Foot traffic in and out and all about their delinquently kept cabin robbed them of all marital privacy. Brother worried.

One day bright and early while a lazy sun peaked over the moun-tainous rise of Red Ridge and as the lovely month of May (Anna's favorite) showers their unfortunate world with her encouraging promise of new life, Brother proclaimed loud and clear in some-what of a surprising manner, to Anna and to all those who counted themselves as part of his household. "It's spring, Anna." May's hon-eysuckle is in full bloom. You know, those with the yellow centers that smell so good!"

Ok, today you and I will go for a long walk along Red Ridge road. You know the old wagon road where you always enjoyed gathering a pretty bouquet to brighten and sweeten our cabin. So trying very hard to avoid raising suspicion, Brother's proposal came from his mouth a mite awkward, a bit forced, but successful. He got the job done.

It mattered none to Anna that it was now breakfast time and already gathered in her kitchen were hungry folk sitting all in a row like early birds with mouths wide open, waiting and ready to get the worm. A very stern smile, quick and easy, right away removed the morning gloom that already had laid claim on her tired countenance.

Brother was grateful for Anna's immediate approval. "That's my girl." His swift smile whispered. He then released the string to the colorful apron worn by his honey and with a strong purpose removed it from her soft round personage. Withholding all delay, he took her hand in his and the two of them together made a snappy get away out the open doorway. Leaving behind them the cooking of breakfast to be done by those who chirped the loudest.

Once the escaping couple had rounded the sharp bend in Red Ridge road, a callosity of red blooming maple trees closed the view behind the pair and screened them quite well from the spiteful bustling cabin that they hastened to leave afield in the distance.

Briefly, Brother gathered into his gentle arms, his beloved sweetheart. For a divine moment their passionate lips sipped from each other a sweet nectar that for too long lay dormant in the bud.

The driven couple struggled under a powerful restraint to their own fiery desire, but consented to a mutual agreement to walk further down the wagon road in quest of Juniper's selected love nest which lay in wait at the road's dead end.

Walking along the rural fare, looking down its steep shoulders plunge perfumed honeysuckle white and splotched with egg yolk yellow bloomed lavishly and sweetened the welcome spring breeze.

But Anna did not attempt to break one stem. That pleasure she left alone to be enjoyed later on her return walk home.

For the time being, the couple's only scruples were for nothing more than to fulfill each other's honorable desires. The gorgeous flowers of the perfumed honeysuckle totally evaded Juniper's sense of both sight and smell. However, one is not to wonder why. At the present moment, he only had eyes for his honey. Meanwhile, urgent footsteps of the two lovers outwit the clever distance and soon arrived to face the roads end.

An abrupt pause drew Juniper's adoring stare to feast upon the loveliness of his long deprived bride. In deep sincerity Juniper whispered, "I love you dear Anna." No words of "I love you too" formed on Anna's lips, but judging from the love that flowed from her whole being, no words were needed. The visual grasp of Juniper's magnificent outdoor manner came to Anna quickly. An earlier mental picture of the natural arbor that he had drawn for her, excluded nothing at all. Every lovely scene came into play. A huge cluster of evergreen pine bearing foliage as thick as conferring moss huddled together while the overhang of their massive branches tangled together and formed a natural arbor.

Against the density of the color green, a sky of soft surrealism closed around them. Beneath the towering trees a thick mat of honey gold pine needles incited an illustrious glow which torched the romantic's pathway and led them into their secret haven.

A swinging door to close behind them, shutting out unwanted guest would be void of purpose. The woodland's seclusion and also the watchful eye of a sun bathing mourning dove whose feet clinched the open branch of an early budding chestnut tree just a stone's throw from the couple's hide away provided a sufficient privacy. An abundance of new fallen needles as clean and pure as the soul of a saint lay in peaceful silence and waited for the harvest. Collectively, the whole of the fine harvest offered them with pleasure to serve as a beautiful yield in Brother's creative love nest. While standing nearby, Brother's bride of five lovely years looked on in amazement. At that moment she had discovered a part of her husband yet unlearned.

Suddenly every fiber of Anna's body trembled with a familiar anticipation. All doubts which for a moment had perpetrated her trusting heart in regard to his ability to properly attend her comforts were now excluded worries. The gratifying thrill returned a seemingly lost pleasure to stir within her a pleasant memory and hastened charming thoughts toward a honeymoon delight. Juniper, III, placed himself in the exact middle of the opulent ground cover of pine straw. Upon doing so, he bent his strong five foot tow, bodily frame from a thin waist downward and flared his small but masculine hands in the fine manner as does the tail feathers of a strutting rooster. Proceeding, he moves the flowing hands over the mat of glistening straw. And, at the same time h is contorted body dances upon the golden carpet like a courting swan dances upon the water.

In great ease the released straw comes together in a large bundle inside his strong arms. Each bundle is then stacked one at a time upon the ground into a very large heap. Consequently, having done all to force the issue, Juniper lowers himself to a half squat and begins to shape the straw mound into an elegant bed fit to serve a queen. As the results of the eager man's animated labors, the mobile pine needles amassed in a perfect togetherness as if the move came of its own self will. "It must be perfect" Juniper had here-to-fore proclaimed. And, perfect it was.

Nothing could ever be too good for my Anna, said he. Of course, this creation was his very best ever. In fact, creation of the pine straw bed was his only creation ever! But, he would not be the one to tell her so. That would be for evermore his secret. So, he thought, "Some things are just better left unsaid."

In a moment, Juniper paused from his labor of love and turned to face due east. He then glanced up into the glaring face of the yellow sun. For a brief moment, a vivid picture of Ho Bo's sunrise which still remained to be painted on a long ago memory flashed by. The fleeting memories, however, did not in any way flaw or burden the present dream. So, after having judged the sun's angle to be a nuisance to the dreamy eyes of his missus, he was careful to place the straw rest angled northward. Even though the delicate matter was of a clear understanding, that although he is very much loved and appreciated for who he is today, Mr. Sun and his wicked tease would be banned from his fooling around with the tempting eyes of his Mrs. A smiling Juniper turned to face his bride. He released the small buttons to his grayish blue shirt and at once removed it from a set of robust shoulders and a hardy back. His firm stance placed the wind to his back. The blue shirt rippled gaily as Juniper gently spread it to cover a portion of the fine pine straw bed.

A moment's glance met Anna's approval. The thick mat of straw provided a pleasing comfort. From head to foot in form it was liberal (in length) but it's width less from side to side than they were accustomed to at home. But, here and now, who would notice? Anna observed Juniper's thoughtfulness with considerable eagerness. The tender moment pleased his women in waiting. So while carefully observing his every move, Anna envisioned the straw sprinkled shirt to be a dainty satin sheet which had been purchased from the mercantile store, and its color to be the color of an early flowering violet.

Also in her immediate imagination, the plump spread of straw bedding came forth as a billowy cloud of pure white cotton and her pillow could only be the adorable Milky Way. Is it any wonder, Anna's heart skipped a beat. Anna paused a moment in thought and breathed inwardly a promise to herself. Let come and go what may, she began; this magic moment shall never escape my memory. Turning again, Juniper, III advanced toward Anna's outstretched arms.

His helpless body once more crumbled into an emotional

swagger. One over which he had no control. However, this once in a lifetime yaw, unlike the forced swashbuckler that he had long ago presented while in a rage of ignorance to the town of Cucklebur, this was no lighthearted swank with dangling hands to the side or a bent sacroiliac; but a natural, respectful, and easy manifestation of true love. No sir, it was in no way akin to yesterday's swagger. She now in her womanly transpose was captured between the twinkle in his eye and the drumming of his heart. Anna never looked more beautiful. Her thin cotton dress which printed out tiny blue daisies wrapped snug by the wind to her soft body, revealed a most desirable women. The once cropped short sable brown hair falls a loose and lustrous shoulder length. Her magnetic charm drew him like a shooting star streaking across the night's heaven. Likewise, Anna stood ready and willing to surrender all. Desiring eyes of the two mates met in passion and never let go as Juniper with much tenderness slowly scooped up the body of the women whom he loved from off her feet then into his longing arms.

Here upon God's approved union, the straw pallet in gladness, past on his comfort to serve the carefree couple while their unrestrained desires in perfect harmony blended just as the foaming waters blend when the sea billows roll.

Afterwards the eyelids of the contented couple closed to enjoy a sweet renewal. And so did the late morning's moon as it slowly sank into the peaceful sea.

Today, much different from all others before restored a previous hope that he feared had been lost forever. Juniper's sweet Anna had offered no obvious concern toward a possible conception. His faith in hope that love will find a way had reached a full fruition. She had indeed made her husband a very happy man. But the wise man spoke not a word.

While the couple's sleep prolonged their stay in bed, a red-tailed hawk made a lazy circle as he sailed miles above their heads in a high noon sky. The magnificent fowl's squeak repressed and lengthened came down for a mere reminder that time moves on and so should they.

Of course, his considerate favor was received as such and nothing more. Anyway, purpose of the hawk's rather mournful call accomplished his well-meaning intent right away. Juniper and Anna immediately ceased their tranquil slumber then scrambled to their feet, mussing the straw bed once made perfect.

In the meantime, having realized the time of day, Anna exclaimed, "Goodness! We must hurry, else our house quest will soon be organizing a search party to bring their wondering one's back to the fold." Both she and he sort of chuckled, but their laughter resulted more from disgust rather than from merriment.

"Come quick Anna," Juniper, III coaxed sweetly. No one is never to share our special place here in the woods and especially our sacred bed. So the two made haste in their wasting of the pine needle. Scatter the pine needle exactly or as much as is possible, as they were. And Brother exclaimed, "In that manner no one will ever be the wiser. The straw will cover our tracks nicely."

"You're a clever man," said Anna.

"You bet I am, my little turtle," said he.

And so while each of their smiling faces wore soft patterns of fine lace, compliments of the dancing sunlight that filtered through dainty gaps in the nature's canopy overhead, Juniper and his honey gave their all to a rapid destruction of an earlier paradise. Together the frivolous twosome kicked, shuffled, jabbed, and poked with both feet and hands until every last trace of the beautiful straw rest had been dismantled beyond recognition. Therefore, following an almost flawless restoration to the forest floor's covering, Mr. and Mrs. Juniper Higginbotham marched off arm in arm toward the bustle of their dear beloved cabin home, leaving behind them, tucked away amid the sugar pine, their precious secret, presently hidden in the lush soul of the woods.

At this moment they were about to round the road's ben that would ultimately place them eye to eye with their cabin home, when Juniper exclaimed, "Anna! Where is your bouquet of flowers?"

"Bouquet, bouquet" she repeated.

"Yes, Anna, bouquet. The one to brighten our cabin! Honeysuckle!"

"Oh, that one," she stammered. "The bouquet, the excuse for which (you sir) offered to our unfortunate dependents in support of this 'gallivant – ta'. " Anna's strange language (witty and preposterous) incited a mirthful riot to the two jolly mortals. Her lithesome body crumpled with hysteria. Both she and Juniper crashed to the ground.

"Get up Anna," coaxed Juniper. We must at once collect our wits and the bouquet. Because the joys of a perfect day had filled their minds and hearts, they had forgotten to pluck the flowers. Consequently the daft pair was compelled to turn back and retrace their own footsteps. And to gather enough honeysuckle blossoms to make believable the excuse given for their reason to walk in the wild. Stems of the wild columbine snapped and popped in a vigilant vim as Juniper broke each one and filled the extended arms of his mate with their flowering perfume. Afterwards he became so taken by the loveliness of his wife and her bouquet, that a driving desire to once again hold her in his arms grew into a crushing blow to the beautiful floral bundle.

"Now see what you've done," said Anna in a playful rage.

"Yea," said Juniper, "but don't know if I can truly say I'm sorry.

Afterwards, following a brief moment's embrace, the giddy couple pulled themselves together and tried very hard to place their thoughts where they should be, "on the return to home and the regrettable dread of an overcrowded cabin." A mere thought regarding their once lovely cabin's ugly mass of quilts and blankets that stacked from floor to ceiling (necessary padding for on the floor sleeping) flashed an unsightly memory.

But because of Anna's great faith in the splendid bouquet that was sure to brighten the drab scene, fed to them strength to move on. And so, in spite of all their hardships and annoyances, together they thanked God for one another and humbly persevered to the end.

Chapter VII

U pon their afternoon arrival, Anna searched the small kitchen and found a large mason jar in which to arrange the arm load of sweeter than honey fragrance of wild azaleas. Not a single resident of the cabin noticed the bruised blossoms but everyone present applauded their sweet aroma.

The lady of the house moved about the rustic room with a mustered ease. First, she fixed the Mason jar filled with flowers to rest in the middle of the center table which ordinarily gave place to the oil burning lamps. Next, she removed an apron from the pine board dresser and in haste, marched straight to the kitchen to prepare dinner. However, much to her surprise the considerate relatives had already cooked and had dinner waiting stored inside the black stoves' warming closet. The delightful look on Anna's face moved the lot of them to a merry laughter and caused the slipshod cabin to hum.

From that day forward the unpretentious caballero known still to most folk only as Brother Higginbotham, prayed daily for a most needful change in current economics and in his own household. And soon, to the believer, a good change did come. Employment relief to the southern states was eventually realized all across the land. Right away, comparable to the days of Noah and his ark, Brother's visiting homeless two by two moved out of sight and somewhat out of mind.

When at last, those who were a little hesitant in making their move, finally did say their goodbyes, it was a happy change. "Glory halleluiah," he could have shouted, but at the moment of their departure he became throttled by a pitiable heart. Thus none other than himself heard the glorious proclamation.

By his calculation, Juniper understood very well just how important were the upcoming events on which his mind would now dwell. Each and every passing day of each month, the hopeful father observed in secret, the pleasingly plump belly of his help mate Anna. His happy thoughts unrevealed to others remained void of note. Yet to the expectant father, every quite moment seemed heart mending. Unlike the change in Hoover's economy, no change in the appearance of Anna's tummy took place. It never grew larger. Nor did it ever shrink. Anna was to her loving husband, an absolute mystery. The pleasantly plump build of her body kept everyone guessing. Of course, there were a few sly tongues among relatives, but no one dared to release their haunting curiosity. Days and weeks moved end on end, in a steady pace, into six, seven, then eight months.

Changing seasons of summer then fall soon rolled the cuddlesome month of winter into an intriguing January.

Still not one clue came to light, to explain why sweet Anna's bodily form remained completely true to its norm. And yet, in spite of constant worry on his behalf, Juniper pondered those finicky things in total silence. So as he grew more and more concerned regarding Anna's tender feelings, he felt that any form of interrogation would be perhaps misunderstood. All the same, rather than cause any pain or anguish to his beloved, Juniper simply held his tongue.

One morning upon the sweet dawn of January twenty-second, long about the moment when Juniper was about to place the blame on God for the lack of a new born babe, Anna's frantic call coming clearly from the back room of the cabin, diverted his unreasonable argument.

"Juniper, you should go and get Doctor Ganus," she cried, "your baby is coming!"

In the haste of only a short moment, Juniper mounted horseback and his swiftness was prompt in delivering the sleepy eyed doctor. And in a short time later on, the good doctor delivered Anna's baby. An infant son arrived on that glad day and filled a long-time void in Juniper's heart.

The little one's arrival was met with deep gratitude. A more ecstatic father the old doctor had never before encountered. He counted baby's fingers and toes. "All there, ten of them." He assured Anna. Juniper's enthusiastic adoration made the doctor's sad task of bearing grievous news even more regrettable. He began by speaking softly and slowly but very frank.

"Mr. Higginbotham, I'm so sorry that it's necessary to inform you of unhappy details regarding the infant, but I must."

Meanwhile with a trembling hand almost feeble it seemed, the old doctor gently stroked the back of the infant's small head and began to explain. "You see, sir, the umbilical cord had been looped around the baby's neck cutting off oxygen to the brain much too long. Just how much damage has been done, I simply do not know. However, I do know that there will be difficulties as he grows in co-ordinating bodily extremities." All the while, Doctor Ganus spoke; he evaded the sad stares of the proud parents.

By and by his weary eyes lifted in a continued address to Brother, the child's father. And as he lay a comforting hand upon his rather bent shoulders, he said, "Not to worry Mr. Higginbotham, there is nothing wrong that will hinder your son from living to be an old man like me."" Going on, the doctor confidant in what he was about to say, smiled and in a joyful tone extended to the grieving couple his brave assurance. "Much can be done to assist the lad's proper growth so that he may enjoy a fairly normal life." He then turned around, zipper closed his black bag, secured it in hand, lifted his well-worn black felt hat from Anna's bed post, bid them all farewell then offered further assistance if he should ever be needed.

Juniper thanked the worn down doctor in a proper manner; paid him the required fee of fifty dollars, then in peace a late morning saw him out the cabin's door.

Once mother and father were alone with their baby boy, Anna cried, "I was too old to have a baby! His pitiful condition is all my fault!"

"Don't cry, Anna," pleaded Juniper. "We have a fine son to love." Tears that would have fallen from the eyes of the father as well were restrained by an extraordinary desire that he himself might maintain a healthy body so as to take good care of his growing son's comfort and happiness.

Juniper's voice then whispered to Anna, "I'll keep my promise I made to you with all my heart. I will never let you down. I'll leave my bed at night in heed to his cry. I will lighten your work load as best as I can. And, I, Anna will find him to be a special joy. Together we will give him all our love and a splendid name."

"What do you say dear to the name, Juniper IV? Do you know what I mean dear? Do you see that it would be good and that he is most deserving of being forth in the genesis of Higginbotham heirs?"

In slow motion, Anna shuffled her tired body upward in bed so that her head came to rest upon the stacked pillows. A very pleasing smile graced the pink powder puff cheeks and appropriately confirmed undisputed approval of her husband's wish. Soon to follow the beautiful smile, she spoke words that were a musical stimulate to his ear. Anna spoke with ease, "I say that would be a very fine name. I've heard from a reliable source that one to three were all fine gentlemen and I'm quite certain that number four will do the name of Higginbotham proud as well."

Brother's broad smile broadened even more to express his love and appreciation to his wife, Anna. "So, Juniper IV it shall be, but we will call him our little June Bug." Juniper III's amusing proposal pleased the saddened mother and somewhat softened the dreadful blow to her heart.

Funny thing how children grow. They are much in harmony with the weeds of the field. They grow wild and rapid. Here today and gone tomorrow. And so the story goes – "June Bug's story". He is wild about horse riding and wild about the bow and arrow that brings down a deer or a turkey. And that young lad could truly shoot straight. Also, he thrills wildly at the casting of an earthworm hooked on the end of a fishing pole. But, quick moves, lies only in the tongue. From the time he learned to speak, he could out talk a horse trader.

Some time when he played alone, he cried in secret because there was no run at all in his muscular legs. No matter how hard he tried, the legs simply refused to run. But right away, he shakes off the unwanted heckler. And at once heads out to go wading in the sparkling waters of the catfish pond. After pausing long enough to give a haphazard roll to the long legs of his britches, all the way up to his knees, he sinks his feet into the shallow sandy marsh then immediately begins the halcyon wade which takes him slowly out into a young boys paradise.

Among the eschewal's many treats, June Bug found that the water bugs were best.

Mr. Strider with his skinny long spiderlike legs provoked a happy chuckle while Juniper's son observed the bug and his weird stride about on the water's film.

Another delight came along with an occasional visit from the southern dogface butterfly. During her flitting flight of here and there and everywhere, she pauses in midair briefly to converse with an escaped dandelion on wing. Born on southern soil and having been adorned in a genuine make-up of bright yellow tulle applique on an earth tone brown tussle, the magnificent flying gem moved about in the fashion she had been born, an authentic southern flower. The astonished eye of June Bug Higginbotham followed every graceful flit. Even though dog face was a permanent dweller among territorial dry areas, she like her fondest admirer loved to roam.

On the other hand, through the window of his soul, June Bug spotted an ugly ol' water moccasin sunning on the opposite shore. But suddenly an almost obscure splash in the shallow water placed the olive brown viper slithering in an aggressive mood across the water's surface. His immediate destination, plain as the nose on the lad's face, warned that it was he himself who was the object of his affection. Straight away, following an urgent judgment of his limited pace, June Bug shouted with an impish cry directed to himself as though he were commanding a well-trained war horse. "Get up! Go man! Here comes the bad boy!" The urgent call demanding a hasty departure soon played out in action.

But certain that his father was out there somewhere not far away keeping watch over him, June Bug wasn't really afraid at all. A chip off the old block, his father who grew up tied to his mother's apron string, June Bug now follows in his footsteps tied at the ends of his father's apron strings.

In reality, by a progressing demand, the boy namely Juniper IV, became his father's constant shadow.

Time unending, disregarding age and manhood, Juniper III continued his parental adoration and support to his physically impaired son. Drawn together by love and duty, father and son were two peas in a pod. Two of a kind, side by side. Over time, Juniper's loyalty steadfast and above all compassionate eventually led the pair to the school of perfection.

By observation many among that particular generation firmly contend that someday by and by, Juniper Higginbotham, III, husband and father will surely wear in his immortal crown a blessed star of grace. But, for here and now he is more content to live as a happy companion to his family. Just he and Anna and June Bug make three in their blue, blue heaven.

As previously promised, in order to maintain a reasonable balance physically in his disadvantaged son, Juniper III carried out the doctors' orders of plenty of exercise; especially that of walking. If good weather prevailed, each and every morning was greeted very early by the father and son promptly at four o'clock when the eight day clock alarmed.

"Rise and shine June Bug." He heard his father call. "The early bird gets the worm." Now that breakfast was done and behind them, Juniper III and son pulled snug their outer garments in protest to the bite of early morning, then the two sat out to traverse the long, winding wagon road which carried them through thick shadows of timbered woodland. A round trip from home to the creek bank and back again turned under foot, five wonderful miles, twice daily. The lad never ever tired of their therapeutic excursions. Both rain and sunshine gave new birth day by day to his surroundings. Intriguing sights, smell, and touch, rising up daily to heighten the youngster's undying curiosity, heaped upon his plate a want for more, more, more.

Furthermore, the repeated wear and tear on bones of both he and his father evaded their attention. Juniper III never complained nor did he waste thought on aging muscles and bones. After all the devoted father was driven by love; June Bug needed him. Neither did June Bug's father ever tire of sharing his son's enchantment with the performing chorus in the forest.

"Be quiet Dad," June Bug insisted. "Listen to the drummer drumming out their toe tapping tune. Who are they, Dad?" Juniper proceeded to turn the volume to his voice down kind of low then replied, "Well, now let's see, but prior to speaking, as usual he took advantage of a nearby tree stump on which to rest while he filled the ears of a gullible lad. After first shifting himself to sit balanced upon the somewhat decayed rest, he ceased the moment to cross his legs for comfort then aimed his stare upward toward heaven as though the story he wished to tell lay somewhere among the gathering clouds. So, following a deep intake of air then the expelling of it, he drew into place a steady focus upon the approaching adlib of his summary. "Well now, let me think, let me think...." The drummers are the red headed wood peckers. They are the rapid rat-a-tat ballyhoo that we hear. There are the blue birds who of course sing the blues. Robin red breast strikes a chord or two while he pulls the earth worm to a taut stretch from the damp soil. Then we by all means must not forget to throw in a few melodic notes of the brown cricket and a whole lot of jangle from the green Katie-did. And, lo and behold there we have now picked right out of the forest a rip-roaring razz-ma-tazz foot stomping caterwaul.

"Thanks Dad" June Bug giggled, "But what's caterwaul?"

"Just what I told you son."

"You sure are smart, Dad."

"Well son, I believe I would be safe in saying the same about you, a ten year old."

Also during the easy living summer seasons, if he should be lucky enough to be caught in a surprising down pour of warm raindrops descending to Earth merely to escape heavens noisy thunder, his day was model perfect. Often during a good drenching, June Bug pretended to be drowning. His screams were always very authentic, loud and shocking. "Help me Dad! I'm really going down!" Afterwards the two of them, father and a jubilant son laughed together.

One lovely summer day as the enthusiastic pair ambled down the country road they came upon a very large worm, referred to by country fold as a thousand legged worm. This curious looking millipede (Aland roving crawfish) sometime cited as a rain bug, but more commonly known in June Bug's territory as a thousand legged worm, moved himself about rather slowly on the smooth tract of his dinosauric collection of legs.

An immediate sight of the strange worm, the young lad's knees folded and he became an instant deposit upon the ground blocking the oblivious worm's escape. June Bug's father in his deep male voice began a strange oral read.

Said the thousand legged worm
As he began to squirm
Has anybody seen a leg of mine
If it can't be found
I'll have to hop around
On the other nine hundred ninety-nine
Hop around, hop around
On the other nine hundred ninety-nine
If it can't be found
I'll have to hop around
On the other nine hundred ninety-nine

Often times on occasions such as this one, June Bug found himself at a loss for words. The mystery of his father's sometime weird behavior sort of confused even him, and yet he was altogether charmed by his Dad's witty lunacy

Of all the four seasons, the young man's greatest delight reveled most of all in the fiery season of fall. Autumn's bursting showers of falling leaves gave him goose bumps. Her magical array of color reminded him of a mighty warrior's head dress and often he lingered among them chanting a playful war cry as if he himself was that roaring Indian. He never grew weary of walking through her explosive splendor.

Chapter VIII

Later on, some distance down the journey of time, Anna's physically impaired son grew up. Now in his mid-teens, he is quite a handsome fellow. He is canny in spirit and powerfully demanding in a stout will to have a full life.

He began to press his father Juniper for a broader and less rugged range on which to roam. It pleased June Bugs elders that they were still young enough to meet the urgent transition from the mountain top to a much lower terrain which provided a more suitable place for walking. So the Higginbotham's soon chose a new site on which to raise a new building. The proper place on which to establish their new home was at last finalized on a very beautiful but frigid day in mid-January.

A light dusting of snow layered the frozen landscape like egg whites beaten into a soft fluff of cream then spread over a mound of coconut cake.

Soon the upcoming month of April released to the fine Kentucky highlands, gratifying weather. A local builder from the growing town of Cucklebur was employed and right away Anna's chosen cottage took shape on its honorable spot west of the singing brook which served as a divide between the cottage and the public road. Anna, Juniper, and June Bug had chosen a marvelous spot situated out in the wide open spaces. There the sunshine prevailed no matter what the time of day. Tiny blossoms of wild daisies lay down a magnificent blue carpet across the open hill side.

Anna was far more ecstatic regarding their final decision than was her husband Juniper. Leaving the mountain that had long been his refuge from birth, tugged at his heartstrings. But, this need to provide comfort for his loved ones placed all things in perspective. Lucky for Anna, more times than she chose to remember, she in silence yearned to live near the county's state road.

Prior to relocating his family from the mountain to its foothills, Juniper III functioned part-time in winter and during cool mornings on into spring as a fire bug to his son June Bug. During school days in session, Juniper arose very early in the morning and bundled into his arms rich kindling and hickory wood for burning. Then he religiously made his way to the huge steel drum once used for the storing of crude oil that he had placed at the bus stop. In no time at all, June Bug's father had a flaming fire burning inside the oil drum. Anyway, upon the lad's appearance, he hastened to warm his fingers and toes while he waited for the Johnson County school bus to arrive. Each and every morning, Juniper completed the relentless ritual of love and then continued on his way to his common work place. Meanwhile the racing fire snapped, popped, roared, and danced inside the black smoked barrel. The grateful boy smiled because of his father's thoughtfulness. A close encounter with the heated metal drum, and a rapid curl of grayish smoke, caught by the inconsiderate fingers of the wind teared June Bug's eyes and surely seasoned his swab of hazelnut hair with the notorious seasoning (dry hickory bark) worn primarily by a back woods fellow.

Oft times when he arrived for class, a roasted wiener crossed the mind of his fellow classmates. Not to worry, the country boy's pride went unshaken. The smile on his handsome carefree face appeared much broader than did the minds of his hecklers. In that area of Johnson County, each school bus made two deliveries. June

Bug rode with the first load of students. Four o'clock p.m. right on the dot, the big yellow school bus screeched his brakes until its roll came to a dead stop precisely on the exact same spot in the road every morning at the exact same time. "My goodness!" exclaimed the young lad, "how can he do that?" Therefore, it behooved him to be on time also. June Bug was indeed the early bird who always got the worm. In spite of his physical handicap, the Higginbotham lad proved to be a very bright intellect and he maintained the excellent grades to prove it.

Prior to settling into the new location, Anna's first and foremost issue must be put to rest; water, the need for healthy water and plenty of it. Therefore, she being unwise to the troublesome mystery which lay ahead pursued with diligence the family's urgency for water. Also, totally unaware of the burdensome load that need would eventually place her beloved husband and son under; Anna's innocents cleared a long and dangerous trail that would lead to a darkened world.

Even during their late date in history, rural citizens of eastern Kentucky were still walking in the footsteps of early pioneer brethren. Modern conveniences such as city water and electrical power still are fainting on the political drawing board. Household provisions for a water supply lay only in polluted mountain streams, stagnant surface springs, or difficult to reach, deep wells. Anna strongly frowned upon any source of surface water, thus by choosing the less of three evils; she opted to dig a well. And so, Juniper rounded up a fine man good in his standing who lived somewhere near their area who was well known for his expertise in that special profession.

A short space later, a yield of the gentleman's dig suited my lady's fancy just fine. So it was, the final wind down of the Higginbotham transmute came to a beautiful close.

About this time in Anna's life, things took a drastic turn. Age and hypertension launched an attack against her good health. Body and spirit alike slowed down to a mere shuffle. Hence the timely departure from Juniper's mountain to less elevation of a lower terrain fulfilled the imperative desires of both mother and son. So although the two lands joined together, mountain and valley, the spread measured only a short distance journey. Therefore, flat land on which to travel is now at the disposal of the infirmed family members. The Higginbotham trade off progressed well. Residing near the public road also proved to be a welcomed convenience to their travel in and out of the pioneer town Cucklebur. Also, the running of errands often brought their remote neighbors into view as they traversed the public artery. While they never ever stopped by to say hello, their lively presence was to Anna a marvelous reminder that she herself was indeed still among the living.

There were special hours during a winter's freeze, Anna and son gained many moments of shut-in pleasure from their dreamy observation looking out the north window of their cottage. Huge icicles, long and pointed dripped dropped from the rocky overhang along the high walls of the roads embankment. Their slow drops looking like magnificent diamonds shimmered in the brightness of sunlight then burst into a million silver stars while they proudly took a non-stop tumble onto the earth down below.

Imagination of both mother and son were totally caught up into the mystic wonders of nature. Anna explained, you see son, we as human beings are like those beautiful icicles. For a while, we live here on earth, bright shining as stars and then after a time, we like an icicle, simply melt away. We also in the same manner as the frozen pop, return to sleep in the bosom of mother earth. Missing the point entirely June Bug giggled, then asked, "Oh, Ma, who are all those poor humans hanging out there today"

But having perceived the expression on his mother's sincere face, right away he tripped off to another room in search of his father. Anyway, due to weather conditions and despite frequent confinement to indoors and forgetting the blues, the Higginbotham's departure from a quiet and serene hilltop of glory to a more versatile plain of wide-open worldliness confirmed a crowning expediency. Life moved forward.

Sweet was the fleeting days of the young June Bug's new beginning. Without delay, he and his father together resurrected the old pioneer wagon road which leads from home to what was once referred to as the creek bottoms. The bottom land, rich and moist that lay along the banks of Wimberley Creek was first plowed and planted in the long ago by a Creek Indian band whom are still remembered today for their late existence in that special territory of Johnson county kentucky. Trailing along for many miles, the earthen road led father and son far out across the flat lands called the Foreigner's Flat. Foreigner's Flat came into community recognition very early in history because of the constant flow of transit farmers in and out with the change of every season.

Most of the idle road had slept peacefully for more than fifty years and as it might seem strange had not yet overgrown with sprouting acorns or pine seedlings. Time and time again light from the rising sun and the going down of it habitually attended the struggling son and his supportive father twice daily, come what may, rain or shine while they traipsed to and fro across the pleasant stretch of Foreigner's Flat. Oft times legs of the disadvantaged boy threatened rebellion to his pace, but his father's presence always at his side had to but touch the lad's upper arm to steady him. And every time, non-ignored, a glancing smile from his son readily praised his father.

Just as Doctor Bently had confirmed at the time of June Bug's birth, with age, mobility would gradually erode. It is proven. And so as each year passed them by, concern regarding June Bug's growing demand for his father's support, their footsteps grew closer and closer together while they continued onward the steadfast partnership.

Juniper enjoyed making June Bug laugh. Every now and then

during their therapeutic hikes, Juniper took time to playfully create the means. Once late in the evening near the set of sun, Juniper suddenly came to an abrupt pause then rushed to the road's edge. Upon observation of the stunned look on his father's face, so did June Bug. Far off in the darkening distance, the sharp shriek of a woodland screech owl blast the evening darkness with his frightening squeal as powerful as that of the whistle of a fast freight train. The eerie call from the screech owl cut right through the dense growth of the evergreen as if there were no trees at all. The bright-eyed lad shivered with excitement. "Watch out, boy!" Juniper exclaimed. "Don't cross that railroad track just now! Didn't you hear the whistle of that freight train?"

"Yeah, right," thought June Bug. "Out here in the boon docks, a train?" And then he laughed at his father's humorous prank. Right away by the light of a rising moon, the jolly pair walked on home side by side, one for all and all for one.

As time moved forward, quite soon, it couldn't have been more than five years later, pleasant surroundings drastically changed to the unpleasant. A horrible night mare dawned upon the contented Higginbotham family. The tragic curse began around the early blossoming of spring's promised reward of marvelous joys to come. However, that specific spring, Mother Nature's promise of happy days was to them almost barren. One April morning, very early, even before sun up. Upon rising from his night's rest, Juniper heard a thunderous ruckus which sounded as if the tortuous furies of all the hades world had broken loose, having no intent of sparing not even community Christians even those who wore upon the gate post of their hearts the mark of the saving blood.

Well, that is it, the end of the world has come, he cried. But, in a moment, with a might closer consideration of the horrible matter, he came to himself and realized that the ruckus could only be the work of man. Kentucky's Johnson county road works had just broken ground a short way south of their lovely home. A state project working toward the widening and straightening of its earthen road which was routed through the mountainous pass referred to as Painter's Pass, and then immediately shot straight to the front door of the Higginbotham's white cottage.

The Kentucky state employees were merciless. Every working day of the week and many times on Sunday, the Higginbotham family was shocked out of sleep much sooner than the day's duty demanded of them because of the rattle and grind of huge construction machines.

The hideous burps and squalls of a giant steam shovel, the powerful strains of a grating old bull dozer, the banging rumble of dump trucks and the everlasting cracking vibe of the road packer all wreaked havoc to Anna's nerves. What's more, there came the rusty rub of a hinged bucket swinging at the end of a long jointed arm that mounted to an enormous cranc, all of which made one's skin crawl. However, above all and worst of all were the powerful sticks of dynamite which blast away and rocked the world as it shook and shattered apart the beautiful mountains. Stone from stone crumbled then crashed to the surface beneath them, sending up great boiling clouds of granulated dust into the outermost part of heaven. Meanwhile, sinking the pristine water contained in Anna's beloved deep well. No doubt, water from Anna's affluent reservoir drained through to the other side of the world, most likely to China, and gives life to China's gorgeous peach blossoms. But, precious little comfort does that assumption give to Anna, because her fine water store is still just as gone. Gone forever – in the exact likeness of the foul winds that blows in madness from the angry old steam shovel. Anna's broken heart also sank to a record low; perhaps not to the far away land of china, but to the very depths of despair.

Compensation for the loss of their water supply came nearly four weeks later on. Those in administrative authority offered to dig another well. The long extended wait for the approval of their proposal led Mr. and Mrs. Higginbotham to receive their promise only as black smoke blowing in the wind. Even should the state department honor the agreement, since previous experiences with drilling failed, Anna's awareness of just how difficult it could be to access a bountiful flow of water from under the earth especially in a previously blasted zone, caused her to fret. Equally, as depressing was the altering route given to the cheerful and inviting mountain stream that continually tripped and bubbled on its way past the front door of their lovely cottage. The delightful brook which flowed gaily over creek rock and sifted sand meant more to June Bug than did all the beauties of nature drawn together and tied up in a bow. Songs sung by her clear cool waters blessed his soul with the promise of a joyous future. And at night while he lay in bed and listened to the rhythm of her gentle flow, he easily drifted off into a calm and peaceful sleep. But alas, the common joy of June Bug's life now lies covered over in most part by tons of crushed stone and fragments of blue slate. All that now remains of her exciting babble is forced quickly through a giant cement culvert – ugly and boresome, which was to the Higginbotham family a progress observed through bitter eyes.

Pure aggravation brought on in the name of progress goes on and on. The already burdened young man met with much difficulty, torn roads, knee-deep mud, and the spoiling of his shoes and school attire, simply to board the school bus. Furthermore, the burdensome wait for a new well to be dug clawed mentally at their trust in promises given by the states big whigs and proceeded to stretch a short wait into boresome months.

Meanwhile, an angry male namely Juniper Higginbotham was persuaded to fill the family's need of household water by a manual haul from the open shaft of an old abandoned mine located a very long way from his home. This oppressive requisition grew quite a sore spot on the good man's hide. Henceforth, every trip his tired feet encountered to or from the distant mine shaft, the grim sore enlarged. Needless to say, by the end of two months, the nasty canker had ulcerated, then, oh my! What an explosion. Incidentally, what more if anything could a good man do? One thing for certain, and that is every fat cat from the least to the greatest who was connected with the Johnson County's road works, stood up and was ready to be counted. Poor Juniper's mortal infliction had at last been properly noted. Not long afterwards, the county's passel of irritant machinery moved northwest further on up the road. And as far as Juniper, Anna, and June Bug were concerned, the busy crew's departure was to the threesome a grandulous farewell. They were thrilled deep down into their boots to share the trifling annoyances with their distant neighbors who lived northward further up the earthen highway and so let the Higginbotham brood never be spoken as being selfish folk. Truly they were a most generous people in their benevolent deed of sharing.

Soon, but not at all too soon following the shift of the work crews location, a hefty built county representative showed up at dawn of an early Monday morning upon Anna's front door step. While he feverishly pounded his heavy work boots against the grassy ground in an effort to rid their souls of a sticky mud collection, he managed a halfhearted salutation. "Good morning. Are you Mrs. Higginbotham?"

"I am," said Anna as politely as he.

"Well, I'm Ned Willybee and I'm here to get started on digging your well." A very generous smile brightened the sweet face of the Mrs. Higginbotham. Mr. Ned Willybee's long awaited arrival had removed the bushel from their burning candle. Anna opened wide the screen door then stepped to one side of the big man so as to gain a clearer view of her drive way. There parked cornerwise to the drive, she observed a huge well digging rig. The unattractive monster bearing all the necessary equipment sat idling. Its vibrating exhaust piped out heavy steams of a grayish smoke into the air. "Is Mr. Higginbotham around?" He asked.

"No sir." Anna replied, "But I expect him to be home around noon."

"That's alright ma'am. We will just go ahead and get the job started. I have a diagram drawn up of the area intended for drilling."

"And so about how long will it take, Sir?"

"Normally about two days, however, that depends on a lot of things such as weather, soil conditions, and how far down it is to the water."

"I understand Sir and thank you," said Anna. Mr. Willybee quickly turned away from the lady of the house then he returned to the huge rig and began the uphill climb. As the rig drove past, Anna observed in wonder, the huge gas diesel generator, a large water pump, and some long round steel pipe. Other things of interest escaped her notation due to the quickness of its passing.

And so it happened, on that day, darkness of rain clouds moved out of site clearing the sky to a diverse mixture of blue, pink, and a mellow purple. The earth's surface, however, remained soft and soggy from previous rainfall. But, all in all Anna counted the new day as being a splendid day.

Right away the fine gentleman sank the enormous steel auger into the earth as near to the kitchen door as was possible for the convenience of the cook and at once began the grinding task that would soon bring forth a suitable water supply. And that he did. As luck would have it, the gush boiled to the surface and overflowed outside the drilled hole in the earth as quick as a wink. Finally, and at last, Anna the cook could sing "happy days are here again".

The bountiful water supply allowed Anna to once more make beautiful her cherished cottage. Immediately an urgent scrubbing inside and out was done. Then and only then did the quaint little cottage sing again.

Nevertheless, only six of what seemed like short weeks of time passed and in a most unsuspected moment, once more up jumped the devil. Water contained inside the new well sank to almost non-existence. Dynamite blasting from the distant construction project gave yet another dramatic encore of their crippling havoc.

Poor residents of the Juniper, III household suffered anew for the lack of healthy water. Discovery of the sunken well water wrought too much anguish to the already frayed nerves of their dearest Anna. Having visited the well to avail absolutely nothing within the water pail broke her weary spirit. She instantly rushed back inside the kitchen. She turned the empty bucket upside down then in a weakening weariness she sat down upon its bottom. Emotions were high and in a horrid mangle. First she wept and then she giggled. After a short while, the two sorrows tangled into a morbid hysteria. Momentarily following their return home, the two fellows hastened inside to see what was the matter with their beloved love one.

"What is it, Anna? What on earth is wrong?" Juniper rushed to his weeping mate and cuddled her shivering body into his arms. June Bug shyly hung back and kept a safe distance from the peculiar behavior of his mother. "The devil came," cried Anna, "and took away my water!"

"Oh, now, now, Anna," said Juniper. "That's not the devil's job. He takes souls and not water. He only takes our souls if we give it to him. So, see now, we still have our souls! Everything is alright, you're just tired. Why don't you go over into Paintsville and visit your dear friend Grace for a while? The rest will do you good." Anna appreciated every word spoken from the kind lips of her husband and soon replied, "I'll get in touch with Gracie."

In Anna's absence, a tried but true Juniper Higginbotham once again faced the toilsome hassle of meeting with the county big wigs which ultimately snowballed into even more and more annoyance for the man of the house. Anyway, after bringing under control a few tempers flared, Juniper got them on the move once more.

On Saturday, late noon, Gracie had served Anna, her dear friend, a delicious launch of mutton stew and barley bread. Afterwards, the two ladies chose the comfort of the front porch rocking chairs in which to share a glorious evening of leisure. Paintsville weather was more than kind and conversation between the two ladies most pleasant. Anna felt more at ease with Gracie than she had enjoyed with anyone outside the family circle in such a very long time. Momentarily, Anna's peaceful lips began their parting in preparation of expressing joy to friend Gracie when suddenly there arrived on the front lawn a hardy fellow, neat in dress, foxy in the saddle, and purely divine. The rider's stern voice toyed with Anna's friend, "Would this be the home of one fine Gracie Dunn?" Gracie sprang to her feet with quite a forceful bound and raced onto the open lawn to meet the approaching gentleman.

The rider, an uncle on her father's side, who by chance came near the home of his paternal niece was afforded time to drop in for a brief visit. Riding down from his home in Vanceburg, Kentucky near to the Ohio River, he was ordered by supervisors on an unscheduled scouting mission in regards to his vocation as a forest ranger.

What a thrill it gave Gracie just to sit and converse with her favorite uncle. The uncle, the baby brother to her father, stepped happy upon the porch and in somewhat of a homemade move, planted himself to rest in the third green rocking chair. Talk among them rolled from tongue to cheek as smooth as one could expect it could roll between one man and two ladies. During those marvelous moments of hodgepodge subjects in discussion, there surfaced an almost forgotten one which could only be faintly recalled by Anna. In humor, the uncle mentioned a man whom he had met some years ago amid his statewide travels who introduced himself only as Ho Bo. He had had a brief encounter with the hobo (as he recalled) in the small town of Woodbridge, Virginia which borders the state of Maryland.

"I too seem to also remember something of a story which pertained to a very strange hobo which Juniper recounted many years ago," said Anna. But after a short moment, the uncle's legend quickly waned because of the lack of facts on anyone's behalf. And so for the present time, the Higginbotham's old friend, Ho Bo, again vanished unending from the lively party.

Anna embraced the uncle's story in the quietness of her ponderings and would at last take them home again to Juniper, III the man whom she dearly missed. Meanwhile, far off across Kentucky country in the blessed land of milk and honey, but no water, the county engineer now employees a different drilling company to drill yet another deep well for Anna Higginbotham the lionhearted. Today, this perhaps will be the most grueling grubbiest inquest ever held for the purpose of probing into a body of the life giving liquid H2O that has ever before been investigated. And by all means, the body cannot, must not, be deceased. Therefore, keep constant in mind the poor family of three weary inhabitants whose happiness is dependent upon its steady pulse.

The fine gentleman calling the shots moved to higher ground to a far outrun past the first sunken well. The rather expansive sweep carried him clunking and spitting way past Anna's kitchen door, you might say, by an approximate count marked off by the spewing and sputtering fellows giant steps, about a hundred yards uphill.

So while the crew of two men, Mr. Martin Lee and his helpful assistant, whose proper name was never attached to his personage, and two eager observers, Juniper, III and June Bug, were hard at work, Anna returned from over the way of Paintsville and from her very nice visit with friend Gracie.

During Anna's absence, Juniper longed to have her back home again. He missed the warm sweet lips he loved to kiss. He yearned for the tender arms that often embraced him, the timid tease of her secret come-hither smile that sent an absolute torture up and down his spunkless spine. And, he was simply lost without the warmth of her feet touching his at bedtime. Furthermore, should one ask of him, Juniper would hasten his assurance that there simply was no other, not one who could put together a cherry pie like his woman.

Fearful of becoming a distraction to the busy workman, Anna kept inside the cottage but stayed always near the kitchen door so as to hear everything that might be going on. One, two, three, four, and so on and on and so forth until the oral count announced the number fifty. about half way, up to the hilltop, Martin stopped and forcefully belted out a frightening belch prompting Anna to quickly close the kitchen door.

"What about right here," Mr. Lee shouted. "Ain't this far up enough?"

"I think I'd go about another fifty yards further!

So, another obnoxious burp sent Martin again trudging further uphill. Once more, the glamorous disgorger counted each masculine stride, "fifty-one, fifty-two," and so on until the counting ended with the even number one hundred.

Mr. Lee, a giant of a man, paused for a moment, breathed long and deep then drove down his heavy work boot very hard against the damp earth, printing out the precise spot where his helper was to place the cultrate bit.

"Now, put'er right down here," he demanded.

"That's it! Johnny on the spot," he said, half-boasting, half chaffing. And yet another rude belch graced his words of wisdom, then immediately the chore of locating underground water kicked off with the fury of a southern tornado.

At that moment, a ten-inch steel bit took a bite out of the red clay soil then spun rapidly downward to create a perfect circular hole all of twenty feet deep before the workmen changed the tool to a smaller five inch drill.

At last, the proper depth had been reached. The workman hurried to drop into its gapping mouth a metal pipe recognized by Lee to be a well casing already sized to fit the earthen cavity which would appropriately shore up its earthen walls was a must. Right away, Mr. Lee fitted the drill with yet another lesser tool in size and again the steady grind began. Then an even smaller opening of five inches spit perfect coils of white clay dust while small amounts of water was poured in by the handy water pump which lessened considerably the machine's grueling labor. Deeper and deeper, the earthen hole continued while Lee, a most important engineer, masterfully interchanged a large assortment of tools. This laborious process, even though mostly a spontaneous reaction on the workmen's part, boiled down primarily to nothing more than a swap meet between man and machine until at last a massive thickness of blue slate rock abruptly halted its grind.

Directly a hammer bit replaced the grinding bit. Pounding noises produced by the weighted hammer hurt even the ears of those dwelling behind closed doors inside the Higginbotham cottage. Workmen of the drilling crew were equipped with earplugs. The sure plugs shut out penetrating noises of the machines and everything else for that matter.

Back inside the kitchen, poor Anna commenced to wring her nervous hands with worry. A prediction of the normal two day's dig had gone over into the third day. Inwardly, Anna cried, "Will they find water at all this time? Perhaps the dynamite has destroyed all live veins.

Anna could not bear the malignant thought of perhaps having to move from her lovely cottage. That would surely be the straw that would break the camel's back. Since a satisfying outcome of Mr. Lee's efforts had begun to seem futile, her fitful fretting caused an

ordinarily calm imagination to run wild. If there is no water, she reasoned, what else can we do short of moving yet once more? Moving
again will break Juniper's heart. And even so, should we be forced to
again relocate, we haven't the funds with which to build again. The
troubled lady simply pulled up a kitchen chair and sat right down
and again cried.

However, nearing sun down of that very trying day, the laboring
of the hammer drill broke through the solid stone to what sounded
to the man in charge like an endless vault. Never before while drilling
at any other site had such an event occurred. The unusual, almost miraculous incident was to Martin a rather unsettling feeling. Instantly
the deep round hole in the ground gushed out pure crystal water.

"Lord have mercy," exclaimed the observing Juniper.

"Man, we've hit a gusher!" Lee shouted. Too bad it isn't oil." He
laughed.

"But to me it's as good as oil" replied Juniper.

Suddenly the attending crew broke into party makers as they
rejoiced over a job well done.

"Well, get a move on," demanded an exuberant Lee of his assistant. Right away the heedful helper again placed himself in the middle of the game as the two gentlemen tied up loose ends to complete
the task at hand. June Bug released himself from the frolicsome few
and ran gingerly all the way down the hill, tripping and stumbling
every step of the way. But by the grace of his divine keeper, he managed somehow to remain upright.

From her station inside the cottage, his mother heard the
blundering disturbance coming from the outside and very quickly
opened wide the door. In his urgent rush, June Bug almost plowed
right through the doorway; but, the outstretched arms of his mother
broke his fall. All the while, Anna's emotional son was partly chuckling, sort of moaning, grunting, and spitting. Between each blurted
word, "Water! Mother! Water and a lot of it."

Finding his mother back home from visiting her friend Grace in Paintsville, made the young man all the more excited. The two-fold blessing presented the two of them with an unforgettable notebook.

At once, Mr. Lee and his hired help dressed what they called the miracle well, showing great pride in themselves and their hard labors. Next, while exercising a great deal of caution in looking out for safety sake, the workman placed the heavy electrical well pump inside the open mouth of the earthen well then properly turned the switch to start.

At first the powerful pump pumped out both mud and water. However, moments later, the stained liquid cleared up as clear as a cowboy's whistle. The big boss, Mr. Lee, allowed the motorized pump to run clickety-clack steady for an hour and fifteen minutes, spurting and spewing air as well as water and yet during that span of time, the water level varied not one mite.

"Bless my muddy britches," Lee chuckled. "You and Mrs. Higginbotham are now owners of a vast underground lake. My goodness man! He went on. You'll never again run out of or even run low on water." "And," he exclaimed "there is enough H20 down there to furnish the needs of six or seven large families, perhaps maybe more."

Three days later, a scientific testing of the abundant water supply proved safe for drinking or for anything else it would be used for. Mr. Lee kindly expressed his pleasure by passing on his congratulations to Anna. "Please tell your misses that I am very proud for her good fortune. The pleased gentleman, Mr. Lee and Mr. Juniper Higginbotham, III shook hands, exchanged congratulation, and promptly each one went his separate way.

From that day forward, the Higginbotham threesome resumed life as near to normal as could be expected considering the frailties of each individual. And although time had heavy handedly thrown yet another stumbling block into each of their get-alongs, father and son were again back on the hiking trail once more and very pleased about it. For Juniper, III, spacing of his footsteps seemed closer together each day and June Bug appeared to be less and less coherent in both hands and feet. Nevertheless, the persistent pair confident with their belief of "nothing can keep a good man down" went about seducing each day as proof of the matter beyond a reasonable doubt.

Presently, Anna felt privileged to wash all the dishes, pots and pans she cared to wash or to laundry all the clothes and linens she wished to or sometimes she just turned on the water faucet simply to watch the abundant water gush out then disappear as it flooded noisily down the drain pipe. Also, a blacktop pavement spread like a dark chocolate pudding, sweet and tawdry over a here-to-fore broadened muddy country road which trailed close to the front door of their cottage came to the Higginbotham family in beautiful form of another blissful favor, derived from their past misery.

At first light of that special day, a new day for Anna was born. She now freed her willing heart of ill will and let bygones be bygones. And, so every frustration and all past misery she gladly swept under the rug. "So, tell me," said she. "Who could ask for anything more?"

Sometime later on, Juniper's regular commute into the town of Cucklebur connected him personally to the merchants and other town's people there. Since Juniper, III had been a sort of long-time recluse living back in the Kentucky hills, with only family and even much of his time alone prior to his marriage to Anna and the birth of his son June bug, his breaking into the unfamiliar world of strangers did not come easy.

Conversation drawn from outside his own small world played havoc with his limited subject matter. His mere existence felt dwarfed among intellects. Much of his mother's teaching and the love of fine words held by his father, Juniper, II, had slipped from memory. No matter, he hung in there just like a rusty fishhook, tearing and bleeding with the best of them and soon replaced the thwarting crown of self-diminishment with a less tarnished one woven by earned respect of some of Cucklebur's most noteworthy folk.

Mr. P. C. Warden, one of those special wealthy merchants in town soon won Juniper's respect and liking. Right from the start or near to it, the two fellows, different as night and day, became trusting friends. Often at the close of the week, usually on Friday, Mr. Warden invited his new friend to travel with him into the adjoining town, Paintsville, to deposit his weeks earning into the bank there. "Got time to make a little trip," Mr. Warden would inquire of Juniper. And of course, Juniper readily replied, "I'd be much obliged for the opportunity."

Every now and then if Mr. Warden happened to be tied up somehow with more urgent responsibilities, he felt absolutely free to request of his trusted friend Juniper, "would you be willing"? Mr. Higginbotham, (always regarding something as important as money, Mr. Warden addressed Juniper as Mr. Higginbotham) to take care of the banking business over in Paintsville for me today? Juniper was more than willing, actually he was delighted. A bus ride gave him pleasure and a reason to further fan out into the larger town. And besides, his friend Mr. Warden was footing the bill. Therefore, Juniper, while holding on tight to the bag of checks, cash, and a few money orders bravely boarded the commercial transit and headed out to Paintsville to fulfill the prized trust of an important businessman.

He was pretty much certain that no one on board the bus gave a second thought to him as being a banker. Furthermore, the money bag fitted neatly inside a very large brown envelope which nicely camouflaged the contents significance and allowed Mr. Higginbotham to breathe freely. Still while seated among a mass array of traveling characters that sat close beside him, in front of him, and at his back, Juniper's tense eyes behaved much like the eyes of some wondering Jew. And so it came about during one of these important excursions that Juniper decided within himself to go out into town and inquire if anyone might have by chance seen or heard of his most unique acquaintance from the long ago past.

So, following the fulfillment of his task for which he came in the first place, he immediately began making brief visits in and out of Paintsville's mercantiles. He even swung by for a quick drop in at the country burg's jail house. Each place Juniper entered he gave a casual run down of the artist who referred to himself as Ho Bo to anyone who would listen. He said at one time many years ago the poor gentleman lived under my father's roof in our home in the next town over from here, while mending from a freight train accident. He was strangely quiet and withdrawn. The fellow ate very little food at any time. Seldom did he leave his room, just sat at his desk or lay in bed. Never gained an ounce the entire two years he resided there.

Although the memory brought out a tinge of resentment toward the hobo artist, Juniper housed within himself a curious need to understand better this mystery man who had left with him many questions unanswered. Anyway, down through the ages, Juniper Higginbotham's thoughts had fallen upon the roguish drifter far more often than he cared to admit. Oft times, he recalled most vividly the late evening journey that Ho Bo made into Paintsville where he purchased large quantities of art supplies. He remembered quite well how bright the silver moon shown down on one he had perceived to be nothing more than a thieving escapee departing as slick as a button with that of his favorite horse and buggy, and faded into the darkness of nature's beautiful green arbor. And upon the hobo's actual return, he especially recalled the huge roll of wheat colored canvas rolling around on the back of his returned buggy. But more than either the canvas or the borrowed buggy, his mind seemed to rest more assuredly on the shame he was compelled to wipe off his own long face. Above all his short comings regarding his dear mother's house guest of old, the unfounded jealousness of his father's generosity to the stranger, hurt most. All for naught, Juniper Higginbotham, III reasoned in silence, could I only make amends, I would.

After a while, having made the entire round of every reasonable prospect, Juniper tired of the search and quickly made his way out the door of the very last mercantile when suddenly a scratchy coarse voice called out from somewhere over near the oil burning heater. The male factor who had summoned his attention, had until this the last moment, kept as quite as a mouse while warming his gloved hands. Juniper's abrupt pause could have turned both his heals on a thin dime.

"Hey," he yelled. "I've heard of that fellow or someone just like him."

Juniper perked his ears. "You have?"

"Yeah," replied the man who was careful to shadow himself still in the dark corner.

"The old tramp dropped off, or should I put it this way – a freight train moving east on the old Northern and Burlington line dropped him off in some big town further over past the little town of Summerdale, Kentucky on what you might think were not on too good a term," the tale bearer then kind of snickered gently.

Instantly, Juniper, III or Brother as he is most commonly known, again once spiked both his ears to imitate two red spider lilies popping up out of the earth in early fall. A short stride moved him backward changing his position a little in an effort to perhaps place him in view of the shadowed stranger. "Sir," Juniper quizzed with considerable eagerness in his voice. "How long did the hobo hang around there?"

Oh, I don't know Mr., but I'm pretty sure the man who took him in could give you the whole story."

Immediately Juniper calmed himself and hoped to learn more. "Please sir, can you tell me more?"

"Well, the way I heard it," began the informer, "the old gentle-man lived hand to mouth as a transit hobo, while riding from pil-lar to post in a freight car or sometimes on top of it. Once he was even spotted hanging on to the last hand hold of the red caboose." A brief but gay chuckle once again echoed from the dark corner of the mercantile. Also, a couple more chowder heads who were gawk-ing around the store picked up on the chortle. The story progressed above the noisy laughter. "You see," said he, still remaining in the shadows. "When the locomotive slowed down at the approaching railroad crossing near that particular town, don't remember which crossing it was, only that it was somewhere east of Summerville. Anyway, during his attempt to jump from the boxcar, the hobo somehow hung his sleeve and was thrown to the graveled ground. Furthermore, them that told the story said he broke four ribs, all on the same side of his chest. Matters none which side, right or left, and he fractured both legs. On top of all that misery, as if that weren't enough, poor man got a heap of cuts and bruises over all his body."

Plenty intrigued, Juniper insisted, "Please go on."

"Well, continued the informer, not a soul was anywhere around to help him, so the hobo just crawled on the ground like some worm and eventually located a stick of some sort, a tree branch , a piece of split board, or something or the other sturdy enough to serve as a make shift crutch to lean on. But he slept there until morning. And at first light you can be certain of this one thing, the suffering fellow leaned himself upon the afforded substitute, then hobbled on his way to seek help. While bearing the wretchedness of feeling sick as a poisoned dog, he sat down many times to rest but finally he made his way to the nearest house which happened to be a very big house maintained by a gracious preacher and his humble wife." From there the story unfolded exactly as Ho Bo had once told it to Juniper's mother so very long ago. And he who lurked behind the darkness continued. "While her husband the preacher was absent from home, his wife discovered the hobo sprawled out over the full length of her front door steps. The humble lady took him in and she and her children attended his needs. It so happened that the generous lady had in her house an extra room unused at that time, so the ol' fellow made himself right at home. That's not all. They say poor fellow lay-up unable to work or contribute anything toward his upkeep for about six months. And, they say that he was as quiet as the dead so they failed to learn much of anything whatsoever about him."

Enough is enough, cried juniper. Totally unable to bear another minute of his tall tale, Juniper halted the gentleman with a stern show of hand.

At once, Juniper interrupted the fellow's pathetic story and said, "Now, let me get this straight, and I'll bet you ten to one Sir that the meek old hobo repaid the nice lady who befriended him by nursing him back to health freely. Oh, I would dare say about two years or so, by painting a magnificent sunrise on the east wall of my lady's dining room or possibly some other wall in some other room, as his honorable gift to repay the family's kind generosity."

"Well, now. Just how did you ever guess the ending," asked the stunned gentleman.

Abruptly, Juniper hastened to exit the building. He carried with him a boiling temper which was fed by an inflamed disgust. He who behaved himself somewhat like an old rooster, strutting and squawking inside had surely had a craw full. Juniper Higginbotham had almost cleared the stifling mercantile threshold advancing homeward when his ears began to ring fiercely from the boisterous shout escaping from the vocal chords of the obscured story teller. Following the blatant lure the tall frail figure moved casually from the corner shadows and into better lighting. He then directed his call straight forward to the escaping Juniper. "Hey Mr., how'd ya,'" but without even as much as turning back for a backward glance, Juniper charged forward to move behind him the anticipated distance home.

Later, having stepped aboard the commercial transit, he chose a seat, sat down and immediately stashed the journey's gleanings securely under his hat where they would forever remain. Anna need never be told Hobo's secret. Soon Mr. Higginbotham would relinquish the large brown envelope and its contents of receipts, bank statement, and sample of Paintsville's best wine to his good friend and business acquaintance, Mr. P.C. Warden, back in his home town of Cucklebur. While home-ward-bound, Juniper, III, dealt wisely with the day's unexpected news concerning the mysterious hobo, just as he had done so many years past regarding suspicions he had harbored relating to the strangers strong affections toward his dearest mother. Those were hurtful and fleeing thoughts that had in the past brought a degree of grief unto him. But, now having been so enlightened regarding the deceitful heart, the flame of suspicion again burned anew.

Much later on in time, somewhere close to ten years, the name and legend of Ho Bo the artist surfaced once more. Through the thriving grape vine, Juniper learned that the mysterious journey of their friend of old had carried him all the way across the blue grass state of Kentucky and into parts of Virginia to what seemed to be his final staging. Legend affirms that kind and honest folk have throughout time, in intervals of two to three years, continually mended bones that were never really broken, wounds that were self-inflicted and soothed battered nerves that were not frayed at all. His dramatic farce, he cleverly played out and no one was ever the wiser regarding the convincing theatrics.

Who knows what driving forces could prompt such drastic behavior in the life of a man? Oh, to be a fly on the wall simply to observe! Or, perhaps to hitch a ride on the naughty wings of the invisible wind! And then, one could more easily cast the first stone. Huh? Or not!

Many years later, footprints of the greatly admired artist genius could be traced in the fiery colors of the magnificent sunrise meticulously painted on walls in the homes of gracious ladies from Johnson County, Kentucky to Winchester apple country in the spectacular Shenandoah Valley Virginia. Further east outside the state of Virginia, no one could recall the man Ho Bo or any part of his latter day existence. Therefore, he became forever lost in time.

Thereafter with the passing of time, Juniper Higginbotham eventually came to grips with his resentful qualms and laid to rest, out of sight and out of mind, the woeful ponderings of the very spitting image of Abe Lincoln. But, regarding the present time, somehow his heart rejoiced in knowing that his dearest mother would never suffer from having received such appalling reports concerning the stranger for whom she had grown to admire so easily.

Chapter IX

(Ten Years Later)

Juniper Higginbotham, III had now grown old. Nevertheless, although eighty-seven years had run him over, he retained excellent health and a great measure of his youth. The thatch of hair as dark and burley as a black walnut's hull had scarcely thinned at all. Furthermore, within the be-line beam of his ocean blue eyes, unaided by annoying spectacles, he could still strike a small acorn growing on the branch of a white oak tree a hundred yards up into the sky. Also, muscles of the once hard working man's torso were kept firm and flexible by the daily walks with his beloved son June Bug.

June Bug who is now full grown himself still gives his father a pretty fair run for his money. But, since his son was built upon small bones and a rather short frame, the labor of love for Juniper was made manageable. And, considering fleeting time and its many changes, no longer were walks of the two men together filled with childish fun and games, but were mostly serious talks that came from each of their own hearts. Over time, June Bug's falls grew closer and closer together, and each one became more and more disturbing to his father. Even though June bug covered very well his pain and made each fall an uneventful one, his father lamented bitter tears in silence. A constant awareness of his son's unavoidable need of a wheel chair ate away at Juniper's sore heart.

Chapter X

Time and time again, since relocating to their present day dwelling sight, the Higginbotham clan had thought that just about every calamity possible had hit them broad side their peace loving heads. But not true. Worst of all calamities yet were still to come.

Early one bright morning, having been called out by the sweet musical notes drifting from the songbird's chorus, Juniper Higginbotham and son were soon to be leaving the comfort of their cozy little white cottage marching out to enjoy another fabulous traipse down the old shaded wagon road when alas, a very stern faced rugged built young fellow came bouncing up the front door steps onto the porch. Quickly, he removed a heavy shining black helmet from his lofty head and tucked it reverently under a very muscular arm. Only the screen door barred the mass of a man from entering. Juniper stood inside gazing out and June Bug crowded his father in his attempt to see.

"Good morning," he said.

The smell of bacon escaping Anna's kitchen filtered through the cottage screen door and led the polite gentleman to a redundant apology. "Please forgive the interruption of your breakfast." Juniper smiled a bit at the fellow's twist of the truth. Breakfast for the Higginbotham three had long been done. And had it not been for the lingering power of fried bacon, it would have also been forgotten. Now rushing on to his introduction, the forward dude said, "I'm Payne Shwal, a representative for the Falkner Coal Company. Our main office is located in eastern Kentucky."

Slowly Juniper unlatched the screen door, pushed it outward and he himself stepped onto the porch. June Bug continued to hold his position inside. Mr. Shwal immediately moved back to allow space for Juniper. Juniper sucked up a long breath and held it deep inside his chest for a short moment and then gently relaxed. Right away his overall pockets seemed to him to be the most appropriate lodging place for his fidgety hands, therefore, both right and left hands were quickly plunged deeply inside them.

Mr. Shwal rushed on, "You Sir are Mr. Juniper Higginbotham?" Having been burdened by a suspicious nature, Juniper's reply came slowly while he digested the company man's silent overture. Considering he had not previously heard any rumors of any sort regarding any coal company or anyone else planning to purchase land anywhere near his forty, Juniper respectively weighted the man's serious disclosure. Also the young man's every movement came under the weighty scrutiny of Juniper's cautious eye. Whenever it came down to a microscopic reading of a man's integrity, Juniper, III, held the winning bid. At last satisfied that Mr. Shwal was indeed genuine in his claims, Juniper freely gave his reply. "I'm your man." But, both resentful hands stayed stored inside the warm pockets.

"Sir," Mr. Shwal continued. "Falkner Coal Company had bought the land owned by Pilot Paper Company which joins your property on the northeast corner."

"I know where it is," Juniper interrupted rather sharply. And then he said, "And you will of course be stripping the coal there."

"Yes, sir, and that brings me to the primary reason for my being here." Poor fellow could have saved himself some valuable breath and time too had he only known just how clearly Juniper understood his upcoming proposal.

"You see Sir, and I'm sure you are aware of the fact that for my people to access the property in consideration, we must cross a small portion of your land. So, Mr. Higginbotham, we need your written permission to do so."

For a moment Juniper said nothing but remained very still. A faint wry grin crossed his silent lips as he slowly removed the entombed hands from his pockets. He then proceeded unconsciously to claw in the thick hair line at the back of his rather stiff neck. After a moment in a serious thought, Juniper cocked his head sideways, squinted his dark eyes into bold beads and asked, "And just what is in this big deal for me and my family? Will this bargain be a fair exchange or is it all to your advantage?"

"Yes sir, and no sir," stated Mr. Shwal. "Yes sir, it will most definitely be advantageous to our company but to you also."

"How so," inquired Juniper.

"You, Mr. Higginbotham, will be supplied with all the coal for fuel you need for your household." From inside where she stood at the kitchen sink, Anna overheard every word of the two men's conversation. Her eyes, sleepy from an early morning rise rolled back in a worrisome disgust. She hissed like a flustered viper to herself. "Here we go again!"

"Give me a minute," demanded Juniper. I need to discuss your proposal with my wife and son." By and by during the family discussion, they unanimously united their opinion. It had been decided that in spite of all inconveniences, trials, and aggravation sure to come, no sound reason to stand in the way of men working to support their families came to light.

Anna's tender heart ached at the thought of helpless, hungry children. Also, in retrospect, Juniper recalled many times and circumstances when good people were quite liberal and understanding regarding his work place. And so the good old golden rule once again ruled the day.

Mr. Payne Shwal thanked Anna's husband with a kind and sincere tongue for his prompt co-operation in the matter and immediately began to place all his ducks in a row. But the only thing with the Falkner ducks was Mr. Shwal's pond would hold no water. Sad thing, his ducks swam on dry land.

"Listen carefully," he began. "We will begin moving our heavy machinery into the field first thing Monday morning of next week. But, our most urgent task will be to cut back the banks of the existing roadway which will broaden the road enough to accommodate passage of our massive machinery." That day seated on the front porch of his small country cottage, the dubious company gentleman painted for Juniper Higginbotham, III an elaborate picture of falsehood. Juniper was in no way deceived and yet he shook the hand of the deceiver in an affirmative argument. Mammon ruled the wicked heart of Mr. Shwal. Love and compassion swept clean the heart of his neighbor.

Immediately, Mr. Payne Shwal returned the protective helmet to his somewhat handsome head and quietly departed.

Right away, father and son picked up the glorious morning from which they had been detained and began again their delayed hike to what would perhaps be their final walk down the peaceful wagon artery where they would enjoy for the last time the magnificent beauty of God's given fairway as they for many years had known it.

Gone tomorrow would be the wondrous pleasures of sighting the amazing wild life such as the surprise appearance of the charming deer, the march of a flock of talking turkey, frisky squirrels scampering among dry leaves, a sometime frightening screech owl nesting high overhead in the cavity of an enormous beach nut tree, and the thrilling excitement of simply spotting a thousand legged worm as he begins to squirm his long slow journey across the earthen road way.

In the beginning of the turn of his world upside down, for a while June Bug became very sad and often despondent. However, in time as road construction boomed, traffic of mammoth machinery at work amused him and so he and his father communed one with the other oft times in the cool shelter of their protective porch mesmerized by the sudden change taking place in their peaceful habitat

Later on process of their hauling derived total chaos and poor health for sweet Anna. The horrid rumble of coal trucks heaped with a mile high load of black stuff referred to as black gold, which ran much too close to the Higginbotham's front door, stifled the lady of the house beyond breath as showers of a fine mist of coal cinder carried by the winds current black washed her lovely white cottage. And as equally devastating was the grind of red earth beneath rolling wheels of transporting trucks whose motion was never put to rest. Day and night the insufferable dust came at Anna nonstop and rapidly wore thin her patience which had already been many times tested. At last Juniper placed a stern complaint with the Falkner trouble- shooter regarding the impossible black grime. "My stars man, can there not be something done about this infernal dust?"

Mid-morning of the following day to his surprise there were (Johnny on the spot) in honor of his imploring plea, watering down the powdery road bed for a goodly stretch of a quarter mile directly in front of the Higginbotham home. A massive water tank transported daily on yet another annoying vehicle, spouted clear water like rain showers on a summer day and immediately brought under control the naughty grime.

Over and over again, distant pandemonium echoing across the blackened coal field itself overwhelmed the enduring Anna Higginbotham. Still and all, a momentary parallel to the black cinder and gray powdery mix tended to promote an easy healing to her witchy woes. It had begun to seem as though the Falkner endeavor would never end. The endless project goose necked into three whole years then stretched far into the fourth. Anna's head throbbed something terrible from the persistent noise made by screeching and rattling of iron clad maggots while eating away the beautiful landscape. "Will it never end," she often cried.

Finally at last, came the close of the fourth year of their eternal upheaval. A sudden hush fell over the entire territory. Every surviving creature shouted 'halleluiah'. Even the foul in the air, also the fish echoed their sentiment of glory and halleluiahs.

Chapter XI

In a few short weeks, near to the end of a very hot and humid July, the entire fleet of Falkner Coal stripping equipment had moved out of the black wasteland, excluding two large machines which seemed kind-of strange to Juniper Higginbotham's way of thinking. And to further his confusion, those two remained there unguarded for at least four weeks.

Traffic of any kind ceased to pass either in or out of the present day Dead Sea. The absolute span of red ridge road once more blessed the fickle feet of the Higginbotham hikers but Juniper and son now cut short the daily walks purposely avoiding an approach to the deserted machinery.

For an understanding of the professionals reasoning, Juniper found himself at a total loss. But anyway, whatever their purpose may have been he drew happiness from their quite repose. Fortunately for the Higginbotham family, prior to the company's fold, Falkner produced a clean-up crew of fast moving young men who washed clean the outside walls of Anna's beloved cottage, picked up fallen debris from the lawn and then restored the earthen road's surface to a smooth sailing for the two men she adored.

Juniper and son had now at last been set free from the intrusion of coal miners and once again were busy pick-me up and put-em down as they traverse the once upon a time forest trail that is presently bald like an eagle and as barren as a sandy desert of its enchanting natural beauty. But, even so, the long-time pilgrims were most thankful for the gift of freedom. But, the freedom was not at all like it had been prior to the cruel rape of their intimate haven. Gone forever was the cool shade of evergreen trees. So were the spectacular pink blossoms of wild honeysuckle and also, the delicate blue of the floor clinging violets. Gone were the sudden visits of nature's wild deer and chattering turkey. And gone were the heaven's green valleys. Settling ponds had now overgrown their common scene. Soft whispers of the wind dancing through the open were brutally silenced, but, still the two companions daily counted their blessings. "We have each other," were always gentle words exchanged.

Sadly, two years later, it would only be father and son remaining here on earth to carry on life's task of breathing. For without the presence of dear Anna's air to fill the lungs was the only thing that now seemed worthwhile to the two lost companions. Golden years as a family had escaped them far too soon.

Anna, wife of Juniper, III and mother of June Bug fell ill to heart failure. As she became more and more hopelessly entrapped inside a disabled body, she prayed to God for the immediate release of her spirit. Soon Anna's prayer came up as a memorial and God granted to his humble child the marvelous journey that she in faith had eagerly pursued. The lovely transition came quietly during the soft march of the most splendid Indian summer. Thus, while bathed in tears from the weeping eyes of her loved ones, she happily flew away in the arms of her guardian angel.

Following Anna's interment, visits made to her grave site brought her soul mate to the fragrant grove of evergreen trees. A place where she and her husband Juniper once lay together passionately in each other's arms upon a soft bed of pine straw created by the submissive hands of an honorable mate. An unforgettable moment that conceived their only child 'June Bug'. Visits made by the grieving pair were relentless. Each and every sunrise met the lonely companions traveling up the mountain in route to the sheltering pine grove where Anna lay.

One beautiful day upon their return visit from her grave, Juniper chose kind words to speak to his son, "Son, for three months now we have grieved for your mother. She would not wish this to be so. We must not forget her favorite words, 'Let come and go what may, life goes on', and so should you and I." Then the old man lifted his aging eyes to gaze far beyond the cobalt dome and tenderly implored, "Dry our eyes sweet Anna, dry our eyes".

More and more the misbehaving feet of June Bug drastically slowed down his mobile abilities. And, by and by the slow hand of time eventually applied a hitch or two to the smart get-a-long of his father also. Repeated walks for the persistent partners grew relatively short. Even so, it was not altogether due to any fault of their own, but rather to the choice made aforehand by those who moved the mountain. Their hindrances were primarily due to the bold dare of a red clay high wall fortress which edged the coal miner's farewell dig that cut in half the native hiker's forest trail that led them down to the creek. The creek known to folk everywhere as Indian Creek was to the child June Bug, a favorite place to frolic, but after he became a man its charm more or less vanished. And, his own understanding regarding his father's present day frailties forced his concern that perhaps his dad's daily care for him would also vanish.

Yet, regardless of the old man's infirmities, he could not forget the long ago promise that he made to his Anna. Nor did he wish to. In gladness he recalled, "But Anna, I'll work my fingers to the bone. I'll leave my bed at night in heed to their cries. I promise to make your load light. Please make room in your heart for if only but one child."

Unfortunately, the wondrous little son was forever Juniper's one and only child. But not to worry, Juniper Higginbotham didn't. He was much too busy gloating, too cockish. He was a happy father. Were it possible today for Anna to look down from heaven to earth, she would be mighty proud of her faithful husband. He had kept his promise in every respect and would continue to do so from baby's cradle to his own grave. But from that time forward, he understood that only God holds the future in his hands.

Chapter XII

One Year Later

One unusual day, along about mid-September, a light mist cold and eerie fell across the whole of the Higginbotham's lay of land. Rising up early in the dawn, which was his custom, Juniper observed the dreary day. Negative thoughts jammed good reasoning and so he was rather slow to decide just whether or not he and June Bug should brave weather so depressing. Yet, following a thorough evaluation of the matter, he called out to his yawning son. "June Bug better get out your rain coat and would you please fetch mine.

So, off out into the dreary drizzle the drudging comrades go, determined to squeeze the oil of life back into their squeaking bones. Cold gray clouds hover close to earth and give off quite a raw breath which felt more like the winter month of February rather than September. The old man far past ninety chilled easily. He drew tight the frayed brown raincoat, overlapping its broad lapel close to his thin bosom.

With grit and gut combined, the two gentlemen began to clip off the three mile distance as spritely as each one's infirmity allowed them. However, right about the moment the cottage fell from sight behind them, an old model pickup truck which was put together in patchwork colors like grandma's crazy quilt pattern, red, green, blue, and white all of which were glazed in eroding rust. One might assume that it was most likely to be a junk yard steal. An assumption most likely to be truth eased up the sloppy road behind them. Juniper quickly hustled June Bug to the far edge of the muddy road, allowing the junk yard dog to pass them by.

The driver, who appeared to be about middle age, bent over the steering wheel and clung closely. His arms long and skinny could have been wrapped around it twice or more. The tall torso rose aloft his concealed head to where it rubbed against the vehicle's overhead. His face which was partly hidden by the tattered fur lined cap that he wore upon his head looks straight ahead during his passing. Perhaps because of the old man's age and the unsteady behavior of the young man, the driver gave no concern regarding the pedestrian's observation. No doubt while in passing their cottage, he had observed them many times before and had considered them both to be incompetent. Little could he imagine just how clever the two men actually were. Nor would he ever realize the brilliance of mind that empowered the two rural trackers. Anyway, Juniper took special care not to appear too concerned with neither the stranger's mission nor the cargo that he hauled in the bed of his pickup truck. He did however; observe a string of bright green beads dangling from the rear view mirror. Both father and son were caught by a heavy splash of muddy water thrown from a huge pot hole by the passing of the old junker and yet, it's driver made no attempt to communicate with either of them. Juniper never saw the man's face and so he could not identify the stranger. Furthermore, out of fear for the life of his son and that of his own, he would not even if he could. Neither man, Juniper or June Bug, even spoke to anyone about the suspicious cargo that lay inside the bed of the stranger's pick-up truck. The two fellows pretended they saw nothing and simply kept on walking through the chilling drizzle and the bog of mud until the old truck rolled out of their sight.

Suddenly Juniper begged of his son, "Son, we're to mud soaked and wet to go on. Let's go back home." Father's words were to June Bug's delight. At once, both gentlemen simultaneously turned around too quickly for the uncoordinated muscles of June Bug, so down he fell rump first and took a sudden seat in the murky slush.

"Oh hello," June Bug exclaimed.

"Oh hello to you," laughed father.

"What on earth are you doing sitting down there in thc nasty mud," teased Juniper. "Oh, Dad, stop your monkeyshine and please help me up."

The moment they arrived home the two mud sops took a seat on the front porch bench, unlaced their wet boots, dropped them to the floor then continued to sit there in sock feet while they calmly awaited the return of the suspicious stranger and his rebuilt truck. The waiting period almost imposed an unwanted threat to their mid-day meal. But, finally a listless rumble impregnated the mornings gloom while the patchwork vehicle dug out its escape through deep cut trenches of menacing sludge.

The front porch of the Higginbotham's white cottage served well to the amateurish private eyes, as a safe harbor and it also elevated the spying pair just enough above the forging pick-up whereas to afford them an unmistakable view of its contents. Presently fulfilling Juniper's dreaded suspicion, the empty bed of the strange man's old pick-up truck came slipping and sliding down the mud-drenched road and hurriedly past them by, giving no heed to their presence. Its problematic cargo had been disposed of somewhere in or around the deserted coal field. A fearful dread overwhelmed the spying Juniper and he thought to himself, "Oh my! This could possibly be the time that curiosity will indeed kill the cat." But not wishing to upset his son, Juniper pondered the frightful event inside himself and kept quiet. Quite served the moment well. June Bug had already dismissed from his mind the whole incident. His forgetfulness induced by a hungry belly brought peace to both father and son.

"Come, June Bug," father cheerfully suggested. "Let's make dinner. I'm hungry and please close the front door. Its draft is bringing in the dampness and angering old Author." Inflammation of the bone had recently become a noticeable nuisance to the joints of the aged Juniper Higginbotham, III.

Later on following the consuming of a hasty prepared meal of salmon patties, boiled egg, and buttered toast, the man of the house, while nursing a full stomach, first turned on the television then laid himself down upon the fading blue sofa which had in days gone by while under the tender love and care of Anna seen better days. Ordinarily he napped at noon and most always missed the twelve o'clock news. But on that day by some strange coincident, he was wide-awake and gave no thought to even dozing.

The first words to come from the mouth of the newscaster's, that is, following a brief "good morning", was the shocking kidnap report of a well know citizen of Johnson County, Kentucky who was slated to soon become a permanent doctor in the small town of Cucklebur. Thus far in the history of the relatively new town, Cucklebur had not had in residence a medical physician. Therefore, such devastating news had thrown the whole town into a prickly stew.

Consequently the old man hoist himself to an upright position and squirmed nervously as he in total silence reflected upon the early encounter with the stranger and his strange vehicle, but even more so upon the strange man's cargo. The golden voice soft but clear speaking from the TV stated that the early morning kidnap progressed amazingly smooth and simple. The very young physician had been taken from the parking space where she waited for the return of her husband, just outside the motel in which she and he had attended a birthday party for a close friend of her husband's. He had left her there momentarily while he returned in side to reclaim a favorite cigarette lighter which he had carelessly left behind. It was reported that authorities found no sign of a struggle. Not a thread of clothing neither a straw of her hair had been retrieved from the sight where she waited. The kidnaper had driven her away in her husband's royal blue Mercedes.

Right in the middle of the alarming report, Juniper arose to his feet, switched off the blaring television and grumbled, "never anything but something bad". So, no news is good news. Instantly he turned to June Bug. "What say you son, we play some dominos, huh?" Dominos, a game perfect for cloaking frazzled nerves and uneasiness came in handy. Anyway, only one game went down and then the tired old gentleman went to bed. June Bug did likewise. However, early retirement did not mean sleep for the restless Juniper. For hours his anxious body flipped and flopped like a fish out of water. Both brain and body ran to the shallows, but sleep refused to give relief to his frustrations. But yet a pleasant slumber refreshed body and soul of the unsuspecting June Bug.

On the morrow, the break of another new day although beautifully fair, found Juniper Higginbotham totally unprepared to accept what it held in store. On that particular day it seemed as though the whole town of Cucklebur descended head strong upon the Higginbotham homeland. Men and women alike were all armed with sturdy cane thrashers and most wore heavy boots and protective clothing ready to meet the outdoor challenge, strung out in the manner of waging soldiers across the slow rise of hills, the low green valleys and the deserted coal field in search of the missing young female doctor. All the while the old man and his son kept silent closed up inside their cottage home.

Fearful for his life and the life of his only son, Juniper had from the very beginning made up his mind to discuss with no one the matter regarding any part that he and June Bug might play in the unfortunate disappearance of the female doctor. Wisely, along with his son, the two observers watched from afar the impressive search.

All day long from sun up to sun down the great throng of hoofs pounded out nooks and crannies and every place bearing the slightest suspicion. Near and far away people scoured the land, the small streams and the creeks to no avail. Neither had the discarded contents from the stranger's pick-up truck surfaced. Finally once day had ended and darkness cloaked them, they all dispersed for the time being and would begin anew their fervent mission tomorrow. On the morrow, the same party of folk that is, with the exception of two or three drop-outs again stormed the questionable territory in high hopes of having a successful day.

Their choice of location baffled Juniper somewhat at the time, but later on after being informed via news media regarding family connections to the coal industry and especially regarding connections to that individual coal field, reasoning of those in search of the physician became very clear to him. The rising sun of that particular new day quickly burned off a chilling mist, therefore, once again the inspiring colors of fall painted the silver pool gathered about them in a magnificent glory.

Today would bring to the Higginbotham forty a simple encore of the day before. Strong muscles of healthy men physically overturned huge boulders that could possibly be sealing over a new made grave. Old vacant buildings were searched inside and out. Abandoned storm cellars whose earthen roofs had collapsed and tumbled inward were manually reopened. Every grotto in that vicinity was carefully probed, yet nothing at all pertaining to the abducted physician caught anyone's attention. By late evening, news had reached the searching flock related to a call made by the female doctor to her husband. The husband stated that the call had been traced to a public telephone booth which was placed outside a skating rink located about thirty miles west of the town Cucklebur. Therefore, the present day quest dissolved and the search party moved westward. The sudden move pleased the old man very much. At last he would be free to ponder the tragic event in peace and alone.

Aware that he himself had a long way to go to unravel the urgent mystery and considering his age and the lack of steam, he had but a short time to get there. And, so he pulled together every inch of the man that he knew himself to be and bravely began to row his boat slowly but surely. Each night following his retirement, he lay quietly in bed charting out his secret discourse. Over and over, night after night, he plotted the ulterior course, but somehow regardless of how well the plan lay, it always came to a dead end. Until, one morning when he began making breakfast for June Bug and himself, something very strange happened. He turned the water faucet to 'on', and drew water just as he usually did to make a pot of coffee. Immediately, his keen sense of smell picked up a very foul odor.

Instantly a rapid snatch withdrew the coffee pot from underneath the gush of water, but then Juniper allowed the stream to continue its pore. The longer the faucet expelled its water, the more horrid the smell. In only a very short moment, Juniper determined the putrid odor to possibly be that of a decaying carcass. But on second thought, he asked himself, "But how could that be possible? Not likely," replied the inward man, "not likely!"

Once a long, long, time ago, he and some friends while swimming encountered a decomposing body of a young lad floating in the shallows of Goose Neck River. The dual stench totally agreed. And so, willfully avoiding worry on June Bug's behalf, his father hid those kinds of things from him.

After a short while, Mr. Higginbotham turned off the contaminated stream of water and then covered the faucet with an aluminum boiling pot turned upside down. His son, the trailing shadow, stifled an approaching chuckle because of his dad's comical cure-all. "From now on, son, we're not to drink or use this water in anyway," warned his dad.

Afterwards, Juniper followed the footpath which led to the frolicking stream that rushed by directly in front of the Higginbotham cottage and washed his hands with lye soap. Later in the moment a brief reflection upon the joyful reactions of his sweet Anna the moment she received the message that she was owner of an everlasting underground lake. She couldn't have been happier. But on that present day, if Anna could have been there she would have been saddened. Mr. Higginbotham bothered himself non to have the water supply analyzed. "No need," he assured a well-meaning peon. "City water is almost in site." And so it was, about a mile or so up the public road, water lines were already in place. Meters popped up like day lilies on the residential properties of rural families.

So, he too laid faith on the line of public water works that at last those in authority would put an end to the problems of many needy tenants; especially for those members of the bounced about Higginbotham household. Right away, Juniper anxiously pulled from the well the electrical water pump, stashed it in the corner, and sealed the large round hole by placing a flat mountain stone over its mouth, then secured the pump house door by bolting shut its entry. Immediately he brushed together his hands while ridding them of red clay and water then his exhausted body trekked off down the mountain pathway toward home, a very unhappy man.

Daily an update on the missing doctor, Laurie Dillworth, monopolized the news; morning, evening, and night. Desperate loved ones hungered for truth. But, in this case truth obviously was double edged. Among those in authority, it seemed as though a clever game of cat and mouse was being played. One day they supposedly heard her voice via telephone coming from one end of Johnson County, then on the very same hour of the day she had been traced to the extreme opposite.

Confusing statements made by local police regarding the pick-up of ransom money, planted loads of doubt in the minds of intellect. Sloppiness of their performance certainly won them no brownie points what-so-ever. And the role played by the victim's husband in the redeeming provision or the lack of it raised even higher doubts regarding reports concerning the actual kidnapping of the young lady.

Perhaps Laurie's open threats made a short while prior to the abduction that she planned to soon expose illegal shenanigans among metropolitan government, buried her very deep. Inside the old man, every news report naming the name 'Laurie Dillworth' kindled anew the angry flame of he himself being in the wrong place at the wrong time and also the nag of his knowing too much. Still, a strong will and sure trust in himself secured the door to his sometime wavering conscience. Also, more than ever before, Juniper's sleep grows more and more isolated. His aged body turned and tossed throughout hours of memories collage. Again and again his mind turns over the vivid recollect of a bodily shaped bundle he had previously observed that was being hauled in the open bed of an outlandish old pick-up truck, and the absence of it when on the return passing.

In ghostly dreams, he foolishly admires the bright green beads. Instead of the string dangling from the weird man's rear view mirror, the morbid dream hung the green strand around his neck. An awful cough erupted from his choking throat and Juniper awakened from the nightmare. Once more his thoughts lead him back toward the sudden spoil of his bountiful water supply. "Strange," but sarcastically he asked of himself, "and just how would a deceased body manage to find its way into an underground lake of water?" Meanwhile the irrational notion played a lively game of 'ring around the roses, pocket full of posies,' then all the restricting barriers to his present mental quagmire fell down.

Suddenly the old man, although sort of vague at the moment, recalled awakening somewhere around midnight during the night before the abduction of the young doctor and faintly hearing a distant pounding vibrating the earth. A sound precise to that of a well digging rig, drifted back from the far north corner of the baron coal field. At that late moment, his eyes were heavy with sleep and Juniper refused to deal with the incident. But now, having recalled the moment he wonders, who was the operator of that machine and what was the need for digging at that late hour of the night? Little by little, truth in respect to the recent abduction of Cucklebur's future physician slowly congregated within the thick walls of Juniper Higginbotham's weary head. Pieces to the unsolved mystery were falling in place. However, now that old age had settled like a western sand storm in his bones, Juniper's frail hands were tied against the physical shake down of Falkner's coal field that he desperately longed to accomplish alone. So, with that thought in mind, he laid him down to sleep.

Immediately he commenced in full force a mental probe into the entire layout of the coal field. In his mind's eye, in a short time the aged Juniper drew a splendid map of every inch of that specific plot of earth. He drew a recent map of destruction another one of God's virgin creation. And he cried, "Tis the difference of night and day."

The old man had lived there in and around that corner of the world close to ninety-seven years. He knew that land as well as he knew the back of his hand. He was well aware of every geographic swag, every rolling knoll, and every deceiving ravine that once lay within the tract's borders. Forthwith, an easy remembrance of a somewhat long broad sector that remained damp or wet even during summer's drought that continued its lay along the edge of the northeast land line somehow once again seemed worthy of his concern. Quietly, under the veil of night, Juniper began an exhaustive sifting of his reasoning. "Could the soils dampness perchance be constant water seepage from a natural spring? If so, the spring would be feeding the underground lake." Even now, long after the earth's overturn, a wet marsh remains still even through draughts. "After all," he spoke to himself, "a water's current always runs from north to south, which in fact would record the underground lake's location to span the entire length of the coal field running north to south then pouring into the Higginbotham deep well."

Momentarily, that same ol' bell rang again. So, once again having proven himself in-depth, a well taught lesson in geography, Juniper now was more confident in his belief that the northeast sector of the excavated property was considered more feasible to drill in order to more quickly reach the upper level of the lake underground. Suddenly after consideration of the total sum of calculating that he had done, his chilled, rippled skin arose from the bones and crawled. Moreover, the strangling choke to his trembling nerves became simply too much for an old gentleman to endure and so he at once dragged himself from bed, put the water kettle on the stove and made himself a strong cup of coffee.

But right away, a nagging Mrs. Goodie Two Shoes butted into his one and only pleasure with her two cents worth and with her cutting scold of 'a nice warm glass of milk would have served you better'. "Yes, yes," he whispered to himself. "perhaps, perhaps!" The next morning when he looked out his window, not only did he view the brightness of a golden sun, but also he saw coming up the driveway a great temptation ready to seduce his shackled tongue.

Two sets of die-hard volunteers had returned to once again explore his already ransacked domain. Presence of the well-meaning scouts created for the elderly gentleman, a much tougher task in keeping to him self the burdensome but urgent secret. However, he solved the problem by pretending to still be sleeping. And, by placing his point fingers upright across closed lips, June Bug got the message and joined him in the game of pretend.

Although his compassionate heart went out to those who truly loved Doctor Dillworth, and he yearned so much to release the impertinent secret that was sure to lead searchers to the lovely body of the slain lady, Juniper's foremost concern regarding the safety of his on blood kin again over ruled his hearts entreating position.

Day by day, as Juniper observed the persistent probe of volunteer searches, he felt a load of guilt in knowing quite well their labors were in vain. Nonetheless, the grieving man was diligent in keeping his distance from anyone or anything that might perhaps be ponderous into his buried secret. Anyway, simply being aware of the knowledge that the remains of the beautiful Laurie Dillworth would never be found and also of knowing that her murderers would not meet their proper reward here on earth gave the elderly Juniper more grief. Weeks later following the kidnap, broadcast news reporting the suicide of an accused killer seemed rather common place to most all Cucklebur citizens, but to the wise old Juniper Higginbotham, the corny claim was altogether hogwash. Along with numerous others, Juniper firmly believed that the murdered young doctor was indeed that of an inner-city conspiracy. And, the proof lay within the pudding.

Present and final years of life for Juniper Higginbotham, who at one time long, long ago was known only by the name of 'Brother', is now not at all in harmony with the sweet and peaceful life that he had once lived with dear Anna. Other than the treasured companionship of his dearest June Bug, now-a-days it seemed to him that fretfulness ruled his world. Daily frustration goaded by worry marked his once pleasant countenance.

Mention of the name of Laurie Dillworth among friends incited Juniper's quick departure from their circle. No matter when or where it came up, a conversation including her name then Juniper always excused him self and made himself useful someplace else. Each day that the dear old gentleman lingered on earth, the mental picture of the deceased Laurie Dillworth grew more and more vivid. Constantly, time unending, a colossal painting of the petite body floating face down in the cold pristine water hangs indelibly forever on the weight bearing peg of his heart. The disturbing painting presents a graphic yet beautiful image of the deceased Laurie Dillworth.

Long, buttery soft, golden-like swaths of sunshine hair fan out in thin straws across slow swirling water. Thick glass lens encased in black cellophane horn rims cling loosely to her ears. Dark blue Keds are laced tight on her narrow feet, rolled down from the top, white cotton socks appear to be too small, perhaps the results of water shrinkage. The stunning red pedal pushers that fall slightly below the young lady's tiny waistline sag almost to the bruised ankle. A loose fitting blouse, white and unbuttoned at the neck drifts upward to expose a white satin bra. But, of all the doctor's remaining attire, a string of bright green beads dangling from her Barbie like neck is to Juniper Higginbotham the most unforgettable prologue of all.

Time slowly goes by, too slowly to meet Juniper's impatience. He grew tired and a little angry because of his undeniable game of tottering. His hands shook, his knees knocked and his stance which had once been as steady as a rock had become almost as uncontrolled as was June Bug's.

I'll not put up with this nonsense, he promised himself, while at the same time he wandered, "and what shall I do about it short of dying?" And he chuckled to himself, "Now", he whispered, "there's a substantial remedy", while chuckling less dramatically.

Sometime ago, June Bug began to notice the steady decline in his father's health. Therefore, hoping to help, he limited his own physical motoring. Some days he sat so much that he felt as though his thin bottom had glued to the chair in which he sat. But, no matter the considerate son did not wish to impose needless burdens upon his ailing dad. Sometime to serve his personal needs, June Bug crawled on hands and knees in order to avoid unnecessary blunder. Soon, the concerned father realized the helplessness of both himself and his handicap son. So, his vanity and pride got the better of the proud father and he humbly gave in to the silent scream, "Enough is enough!"

It happened during the veil of a late night's darkness while son

June Bug slept. On paper, the old man penned a beautiful prayer in which he gave thanks to his God in heaven for all his earthly blessing, especially for the gift of a son for whom he had once humbly implored of sweet Anna to bear. Then in a brief pause, to reflect upon those long ago words, "Please Anna, make room in your heart for only but one," brought tears to his eyes and a smile to his face. That same hour of the night, Juniper Higginbotham, III, died bearing regrets of leaving June Bug to bear alone the burden of guilt in regard to their secret concerning Laurie Dillworth. Or could it have been that June Bug really did not conceive any truth pertaining to the unfortunate event? Never did the mention of her name enter into any discussion what-so-ever between the two of them. Perhaps and it is most probable that June Bug had ultimately been spared the undue millstone.

Two days later, following the passing of his father, June Bug and relatives close and distant, traveled from their homes across country. Also, neighbors and friends gathered together and carried him to the top of his mountain and the lovely sheltering grove of evergreen pines. There they laid him down to rest once again in the arms of his precious wife, Anna.

June Bug sadly returned to the neat little cottage and remained there nearly a month. A rolling chair was provided him by relatives who in no way replaced his father's tender care. In a few weeks after the interment of the body of his father Juniper, June Bug received a proposal via postal service from a distant cousin who grew up in the state of Maine. She was presently a student attending the University of Kentucky and was in pursuit of a house near the school to live in. Through another cousin who had attended the burial of Juniper Higginbotham, III, she had heard about the present day pickle in which June Bug had been entrapped. She herself, a budding researcher of genealogy needed other than a place to live, she needed also a traveling companion to accompany her personally out into questionable territory while in quest of grave stones and old deserted home steads. The proposed arrangement seemed beneficial to both parties. Therefore, doubting that there would be a better offer or even another offer of any kind at all for that matter, he was quick to reach a fair conclusion, "It will surely be worth a try." Right away, the anxious June Bug responded to the young student's request and the ball got rolling. After a while, the young lady's first class assignment as a research intern required that she grow on pages her own family tree.

How fortunate was she to have at her fingertips a young man so rich in family history. Growing up at the feet of his father, whose store continually spilled over with genealogy and family history, June Bug acquired an abundance of knowledge; abundant enough to actually fill a book. June Bug's cousin, three times removed, began at once the assignment by first researching the three charming crawfish dabblers who resided long ago in the Louisiana bayou; Commodore and his spouse Prudence Higginbotham were pioneers of June Bug's recollection. Also in his estimation, they were most prominent in courage, character, and color of all Higginbotham lineages. Anyway, it was they and their attractiveness that carried the promising genealogist off to her first rendezvous with the wild unknown. Not to mention thorns, thistles, sage brush, and saw briers which eagerly wait in silence for to feast on the tender skin and fine clothing of the poor innocent child from the balmy state of Maine. Although her travel companion still grieved the recent passing of his dad, the female student had reinstated a small measure of happiness.

In the morning of the following day, the adventurous pair arose to kick off her first day of a three-day school break. An absolute strange diet was fed to June Bug that day, but sat unusually well on his plate. Up until now, the pampered fellow from Cucklebur, Kentucky had been served soft foods only. However, this new and different grub consisting of a rare adventure did indeed dish out a real mean cuisine. Only once before prior to this moment had the rural gentleman been beyond the boundaries of his own home town of Cucklebur. When still a teenaged lad, he accompanied his father into Paintsville on an errand for the fine mercantile gentleman, Mr. P.C. Warden. Other than that one tour, he was content and happy at home looking after his mother.

Over time Maine's wild one and new companion to June Bug Higginbotham, followed quite a few leads to their dead end. But, today a different and rewarding steer directed the genealogical pair inland to the city of Richmond, Virginia, a big hop to leap for the country boy. Nevertheless, from the city library she and distant cousin June Bug followed their lead to the banks of the famous James River and then on to the confluence of Falling Creek near Drewry's Bluff where near the creek bank they discovered a small plot of grave sites numbering thirty-six that lay long and narrow across a peaceful, sunny hillside. Although the distance travel carried the duo far out into a rural country, for the most part, the little cemetery had been well maintained.

The student genealogist retrieved a folding chair from her vehicle and placed it at the south end of the rural graveyard and then assisted June Bug to sit where he would enjoy the charming outdoors while she searched the premises. Then at once the thrilling exploration began. Carefully, she examined every grave marker in site for the name Leondidus Higginbotham. Legibility of some stones slowed down her mission. However, one stone at a time led her quest directly to midway of the cemetery and immediately to the moss marred stone engraved 'L. Higginbotham'. Filled with a gratifying excitement, the giddy girl called loudly to cousin June Bug, "I found it. I found it!"

"Good for you," he yelled back.

Quickly she moved to the old granite marker placed to the left of Leondidus and read 'Maggie Devoe Higginbotham, wife of

Leondidus Higginbotham." Soon having had gathered sufficient documents, she raised her small personage to stand erect. Her eyes moved spontaneously afield. Right away, an exquisite marble stone covered over part way with sage brush and saw briars caught her attention. It stood very tall in the eastern corner of the hillside burial grounds. The name she discovered engraved in very large and bold lettering instantly broke open the door to her memory bank and awakened a long ago sleeping legend, 'Fullerton? Fullerton!' Right away the young lady hastened back to her automobile, failed to acknowledge cousin June Bug in any way as she rushed past him, opened the hatch door and picked up a tool to assist in the clearing away of some of the clinging briar vines from the huge stone. The name 'Fullerton', stood alone. No birth or death dates, no words of comfort or farewell. So while she hacked away at the bramble, she wondered, could this possibly be the gravesite of the legendary 'Ho Bo'? Or maybe it could be some member of his unknown family.

At last a cleared pathway leading to the reverse side of the head stone gave the reply to her bewilderment. A simple engraving, Hobo seemed to smile back at her. Evasive he chose to be in life and so also in death does his mystery follow. The marble stone itself suggested great wealth. None of which the hobo possessed, or did he? Anyway, such an extravagance to mark the burial plot of a pauper seemed inappropriate.

Suddenly the young lady remembered her companion, June bug, who waited on the opposite end of the cemetery. "June Bug, I've discovered the head stone of your father's friend Hobo! Can you believe it?" The two companions laughed, shouted and shuffled their shoulders in a rather childish exuberance. Soon following the settling down from their jubilee, the female student proceeded on with the breakthrough to the adjoining gravestone. "Whoopee," she exclaimed. "How beautiful," she shouted as she stripped from the enormous pink stone a part of its weedy wrap. It too was elegant and massive. Once rid of the entire entangled bramble, the pink marble equal in value to that of Ho Bo's stone, revealed a most enchanting engraved image of the rising sun. The meticulous work which could have been the work of none other than that of the artist Fullerton, etched the grand marble from top to bottom with nothing more than the brilliant sunrise.

Chapter XIII

Mixed emotions vexed the hopeful student regarding the long day's work. But, aware of how priceless were the historical findings, she gathered them all together, and then she and cousin June Bug began the journey toward home. During the return drive down the rocky country road, and running parallel closely to the long fence row, the young lady at the wheel stared intently up ahead. Through thin rows of tall corn fodder drying in the field, she observed the remains of a very old farmhouse. Out back an elderly lady penned an assortment of dish towels to a sagging clothesline. Suddenly a thought occurred to her that this person could perhaps be someone well versed regarding those who were buried in the nearby cemetery. Quickly, she stopped the car, opened the door and hopped out.

"Where are you going," called June Bug.

"Sit tight cousin, I'll be back shortly." Stepping cautiously, June Bug's cousin walked from the front of the house around to the back side of the run down structure and approached her target, which had at the moment dropped the pinning of wet towels and had instead penned a watchful eye to the oncoming student.

"Good evening ma'am," spoke the researcher.

"Just one more towel to pin, Missy, then I'll be right with you," came the reply. Exactly as promised, the last dripping towel stretched from the clothes line, the line then hoist high into the sky with a pole prop, and then the elderly lady picked up her wicker basket and began to slowly move toward the visitor.

"How can I help you, missy/"

"My cousin and I have been visiting the little cemetery and I wondered if you might know anything about those buried there?"

Smiling, the little old lady replied, "Spec I ought to. Been living here on their doorstep for sixty-five years. Which'em you interested in child?"

"Well, ma'am, I've very much intrigued with the massive pink stone."

"You and a couple hundred more," snapped the old lady.

"Oh my, Ma'am, I'm very sorry," said the student. "I didn't mean to be a presumptuous bother."

"Well don't be." And immediately the original sweet smile returned to grace the sparkle of her eyes and restored hope to the presently shocked young lady. "Well, missy, I don't know about you but I think I've done growed tall enough, so come on in and set down." The weathered porch swing, a familiar sight in her line of work offered pleasure to the pair and took a load off their feet. Promptly an eager twinkle in the eye of the aged lady blew the cover on the previous outburst. She scarcely could restrain her cunning tongue from the telling of her favorite story.

"Pink....pink, but wait a minute missy, the story has it's beginning with the grave marker on the left, the huge pearl stone, the one everybody around these parts calls Ho Bo's mountain. He was a man known only as Fullerton, no given name. In fact, nobody ever really made his acquaintance. Least that's what's told around here. Anyway, legend goes like this.....down the road about two mile from here, a ragged, dirty old hobo stumbled into the old Tom Wiley farm which at the time was being leased to a share cropper. Oh! I forget his name. Did know once, but now I forget, got lost over time. Poor ol' hobo bare made it to the doorstep when he fell down head- first long way straight up the doorsteps. The women living there heard the ruckus, took mercy on him and took him in. It was told that he had fallen from a moving freight train down around the switch crossing of the Old Southern tracks, tracks long gone many years. There weren't a soul there to help him and so all alone he managed in some way, the way only the Lord knowed, to drag his battered body as far as to reach the Wiley place before he collapsed. Story goes that he suffered broken bones, cuts, and bruises pretty near all over his long skinny body. It has always been reported that the stranger looked exactly like that famous President. Oh, what's his name? You know, the one who read by the light of a burning pine knot."

"Abraham Lincoln," cried the researcher.

"Yeah, Abe Lincoln. Folks say that the old hobo was quite as a tomb, ate like a bird, and never left his room. The pitiable sight of him gave kids the willies. Even so, he lived there in the Wiley house close on for two years while he healed. nothing was expected of him considering his bad injuries and starvation. Somewhere down the line, it was told on the ol' fellow that when he got well, he run off taking the oldest Wiley girl with him, but that weren't so." She paused to wipe from her face a silly grin, giggled, then whispered, "Ah, you know how tales get started always somebody to mess up the truth."

Meanwhile, outside sitting in the vehicle poor June Bug squirmed in his uncomfortable confinement. Although the distance from his position to the porch swing was quite far, he could very well conclude that his cousin's visit would be rather extended. For a moment's entertainment, he turned on the radio, but little good did that do for his aching backside. Meantime, a sly over the shoulder glance toward her raspberry red Rangler and the drawn expression on the face of poor June Bug, beckoned an immediate return. But, she felt compelled to linger on until the story ended. An abrupt departure prior to the conclusion would be rude and was likely to hurt the feelings of her cordial hostess. And so the entrapped researcher inwardly pleaded, "Hold on cousin, please hold on."

Yesterday's ripened tale of tales flowed generously while assumed air struggled through the flare of nostrils and then provoked by nothing more than habit, she reached out for a double take. "A big ol' picture of nothing but the sun," whispered the content lady. "Painted on the bare wall itself, I did know which room, but time took that away from me, paid off the merciful custodians in full for their years of kindness. Twas nothing but a picture, but I'm told it was mighty pretty. Folk around here say that picture hung there till the old house burned. People from miles around come by to look at it as long as the house stood on its foundation."

Rather abruptly, the nice lady paused, brushed her hands together, pulled a very wrinkled handkerchief from the pocket of her soft apron and began to bath her dry lips. 'Missy', as she now had been dubbed, rushed in and took the opportunity to get a word or two into the one-sided conversation. "So ma'am, it was then during the burning of the Wiley house that Ho Bo died?"

"Oh, no, Missy, it was sometime later than that. Yes, it was but a little later on after he moved off the Wiley farm that he rented for himself; rented or squatted? Who knows," she chuckled, "an old deserted creek bank house owned by old man Tully Simpson, across on the other side of Falling Creek, straight over from the grave yard. Of course, ain't there no more. Legend still holds that even up to now that the strange feller lived there alone. Didn't own nothing atall to get'em from one place to the other 'cept in a flat bottomed fishing boat made outta wood and even that stayed sunk under water half'in the time.

"But no matter, they say that funny man visited nobody nor did he welcome a visit from nobody. Now, ain't that pitiful?" 'Missy' gave no reply. How could she? The story teller allowed no space for input.

"Two weeks after he landed into the Simpson shack, sighting of the two grand stones were reported by a traveling man who passed through the community from over near Drewry's Bluff. Long ago them poor folk who lived back then thought that they simply popped up right outta the ground just like two sprouten' mushrooms." Both she and 'Missy' laughed out loud. Neither could conceive such ignorance.

"Upon their arrival to the present location, the two stones were in perfect form, eloquently polished and untouched by chisel, riffler, or rasp. Stunning flecks of pink gave to the one stone a prestigious aura like that of a pink rose. The other, a pearly white mound rose up to speak a language of royal significance. The pair of marble gems was as smooth as glass and together a glittering shower of light mingled like star dust while falling to the ground around them.

"Not long following the sighting, eerie screams, resentful of the piercing chisel, shook the night. Work of the artist took place most often by moonlight, but an oil burning lantern served as light during absence of the moon; or, so implied the legend. Notwithstanding, it was by the light of day that inquisitive spies kept close tabs on the work in progress. Daily born were a few letters at a time and then overnight there upon the face of the pearly mound the name 'Fullerton' appeared. Next on the opposite side of the giant marker, the surprised inscription 'Ho Bo came to life'. Also and finally, after many months of meticulous creativity, the lovely pink gem wore an embellishing engraving of the sun rise."

"But a few nights prior to the completed work of art, a group of brave young men sat out in the darkness in hopes of witnessing whoever the engraver might be. However, an unpredicted intrusion of Mother Nature placed a tight fitting cork into their tasty bottle of wine. A summer gale sneaked in, bringing as her guest rumbles of thunder, blue flaming lightning and flash floods which ceased their mischief. By and by, prior to escaping a bright light turned on by a bolt of lightning, presented to the drenched party, a real life ghost! The ghost of a man stood a brief right and between the two stones. He appeared very gangly. His bare head lay loosely back as his long arms reached for the sky. His face, glazed over by the down pore of water, smiled. Rain flowing over him so heavy and thick made of him a waterfall. The horrific image reflected in the tall pristine pearl. First sight of the frightening ghost dissolved their bravery then, a blind scramble of bodies crashed them altogether into one big roll down the mountain." The elderly lady wrinkled her nose into a bit of a sneer and whispered, "Now, 'Missy', I know what you're thinking, but you're dead wrong."

The traveling duo stayed over one more night allowing 'Missy' to visit with distant neighbors in anticipation of perhaps gathering the finish to Ho Bo's intriguing story. Lucky enough that she did.

Chapter XIV

Fullerton descended from a family of artist somewhere up in the New England states. His great grandfather, the proprietor of a thriving railroad company once owned an entire fleet of steam driven engines. From childhood forward, Fullerton dreamed of someday walking in the footsteps of the great artist, 'Norman Rockwell'. He too longed to charm the world with carefree depictions of real life accounts. However, while in his prime still, he replaced the passionate dream with a marriage to a very gorgeous yet mischievous young woman.

Fullerton's amorous love for this dewy knockout led him immediately down the path of deception. He believed that the sun rose and set with her beauty. But, alas, a young man much more handsome than he, armed with glittering gold dangled before the disquieted eyes of his lovely bride, an immediate feast of glamour and the foolish maiden embraced the flowery appeal. Then while riding on the shirt tail of only a three month espousal to husband, Fullerton, the beautiful bride and her handsome lover in secret ran away. Certain that without his life giving bride, peace on earth for him would be unreachable. Consequently, the self-made promise of redemption in time became a reality. The clever cover of a hobo led him freely up and down the universe. From coast to coast, and mountain to mountain, an ever jealous revenge fed to the salty shrew, a burning desire to find the escaped bride regardless of cost here on earth or in the unknown world to come.

One afternoon late on the eve of the ghostly incident, two or three days removed, a fisherman discovered the buzzard riddled remains of the man called Ho Bo. Tacked to the primitive door of the shanty which clung to the upper banks of Falling Creek, in which the hobo was known to reside, a note written in the eloquent penmanship of the self-taught artist, although spattered by the elements and decayed flesh of Mr. Fullerton, remained legible.

She was to me, the rising sun.
In the lack of her smile, I have floundered
helplessly in the dark.
But now I am contented.
At last I bask in the sunshine of her smile.
I am warmed by her blood.

Fullerton's remains were promptly recovered and entered in the shadow of his mountain.

Upon taking leave of the Falling Creek community, 'Missy', the university student paused for a moment's reflection. She spoke gently to her most valued companion. "June Bug," said she, perhaps you and I shan't pass this way again, but this one thing I am certain of. My heart will return here again and again." And so, having bagged the community gold, the fair student and her handyman friend faced the sore task of motoring the long journey home. On their way, 'Missy' never tired of chattering. But, the tightly bound nerves of the poor entrapped passenger, baked entirely done, heated by the fiery tongue. All the way home Ho Bo and the never ending story beat down like rain. At last the Rangler's head lights picked up Anna's fading cottage. Once adored by her only son, June Bug right away weeps from the sight of it. No longer does he regard its comfort, but he now longs to join his loved ones. Day by day, a joyless life withered the lonely man's contentment. By and by the cherished son, born to the union of Anna and Juniper Higginbotham, III, willed himself to die.

Food and drink lay bitter on his tongue. The brightness of each daybreak blinded his eyes. And so, early one morning upon her rising, his faithful cousin and friend, discovered the peaceful body of Juniper, IV lying cold in bed. One day later, somewhere near to ten o'clock in the morning, on the hill top, a mournful turtledove who called from beyond the way of a flowering cottonwood tree, directed the hearts of the few friends and kin folk who gathered together to witness the sweet interment of the deceased body of a triumphant citizen who had resided all his many years a short distance outside the small town of Cucklebur, Kentucky.

The physically impaired remains of Juniper Higginbotham, IV, returned to forever more rest upon the exact same portion of earth on which he had been conceived. And, just as intended in the long, long, ago by Juniper and his dear wife, Anna, on that special day, no trace of the couples' sacred bed of straw, once formed on the ground by loving hands of Juniper, III, came to light. It too now lays molding in the clay.

June Bug, nevertheless, sleeps in peace while nature lays over his bed of clay, a soft sienna blanket woven over time from the arbors slow decent of pine needles. Meantime, dust of the beloved three, the soil, the planter, and the seed together make up a perfect blend of earthen immortality.

So at the going down of an evening sun from the new made grave there arose a cool, gentle vapor bearing a serene whisper.

"Home."

And it feels like I've never been gone.

The End

CPSIA information can be obtained at www.ICGtesting.com
Printed in the USA
LVOW10s1938151015

458475LV00001B/81/P